Praise for the Story o
Dark Secret Love and T

"Alison Tyler delivers sex scenes brimming with breathless intensity, marrying them with the deep emotions and irresistible desires that fuel her character's kinky journey of self-discovery."

—Barbara Pizio,
Executive Editor of *Penthouse Variations*

"Readers tired of sensationalistic portrayals of BDSM will appreciate Tyler's nuanced and realistic approach."
—*Publishers Weekly*

"*Dark Secret Love* is derived from the personal longings and desires from the author's colorful palette of sexual experiences."

—New York Journal of Books

"Providing candid revelations of her BDSM lifestyle (and based on her personal journal recordings), Alison Tyler draws upon some twenty-five years' experience as a gifted author of erotic literature to create what must be described as a kind of docudrama that commingles personal experiences with a novelist's vivid imagination. The result is a compelling read from first page to last!"

—Midwest Book Review

"*Dark Secret Love* could be a roadmap for other uninhibited young women, a trip down memory lane for older submissives, and escapist fantasy for the curious among us; any way you read it, this book is a lot of fun."

—xoxoamore

"If you're tired of the dozens of stories that whitewash BDSM—tales where the sub has more orgasms than stripes, where the first Master who recognizes her as a 'natural submissive' turns out be her soul mate, where her fear disappears with the first mild slap on her bare ass—check out this book. Ms. Tyler makes it clear that being a submissive isn't necessarily easy. It's a process of growth."

—Erotica Revealed

"The kinky, red hot sex practically drips off the page in *Dark Secret Love*. Alison Tyler has created an erotic masterpiece! Be warned—once you start reading it'll be hard to stop until you reach the book's climax."

—Rachel Kramer Bussel,
editor of *The Big Book of Orgasms* and
Cheeky Spanking Stories

"*Dark Secret Love: A Story of Submission* is not a story but a journey. I was expecting a story and was blown completely away...This book is not just well written but the ring of authenticity is striking."

—Cocktails and Books

"Alison Tyler's name will be known to anyone who has read more than one piece of erotic fiction. An accomplished editor, authoress and now publisher with Pretty Things Press, she writes with a fun-loving style that is instantly recognizable and easy to enjoy. And, although she's been writing prolifically for more than a decade, there is no trace of any weariness in her work. Each line reflects the cheerful anticipation of a yearned for promise."

—Ashley Lister,
Erotica Readers & Writers Association

"Finally, we have an erotic novel that steers clear of the ingenue-to-goddess trope in a delightful return to old-school erotica."

—*Romantic Times*

"In a novel that blurs the line of memoir and metafiction, *The Delicious Torment* explores the darker emotions that are often so transfixing in Tyler's work: shame, jealousy, self-discovery, even finding empowerment as a sub explores the role of the dom, revealing ever more tantalizing glimpses into the BDSM relationship dynamic. Fiction, semi-biography, or meta, it doesn't matter. Alison Tyler shines as a literary voice in erotic fiction."

—City Book Review

"One of the leading contemporary authors of erotica long before the E. L. James tsunami, American writer Tyler also explored when younger many of the dangerous detours of the BDSM world in her real life and, until now, had only documented this in her blog…Written as thinly fictionalised biography, this is both fascinating, scary and heartfelt but also profoundly humane, and shows that the unsettling quirks of the human mind and body can come in much more than fifty shades."

—Lovereading.UK

"This coming-of-age story sees lead character Samantha entwined with an older man, a bondage connoisseur and her equal in every way, as she explores her master's desires and her heart."

—*Adult Video News*

"There are plenty of SM books out there now, but nobody does it with as much style and skill as Alison Tyler."

—Sacchi Green, editor of *Wild Girls, Wild Nights*

"A brilliantly crafted and well-written story. I love the honesty in this series...it is what it is, and I love it!"

—Laila Blake, author of *By the Light of the Moon*

wrapped around your finger

Also by Alison Tyler

A Is for Amour
Afternoon Delight
B Is for Bondage
Best Bondage Erotica
Best Bondage Erotica, Volume 2
The Big Book of Bondage
C Is for Coeds
Caught Looking (with Rachel Kramer Bussel)
D Is for Dress-Up
Dark Secret Love
The Delicious Torment
E Is for Exotic
Exposed
F Is for Fetish
Frenzy
G Is for Games
Got a Minute?
H Is for Hardcore
The Happy Birthday Book of Erotica
Heat Wave
Hide and Seek (with Rachel Kramer Bussel)
Hurts So Good
I Is for Indecent
J Is for Jealousy
K Is for Kinky
L Is for Leather
Love at First Sting
Luscious
The Merry XXXmas Book of Erotica
Morning, Noon, and Night
Naughty or Nice
Never Have the Same Sex Twice
Never Say Never
Open for Business
Playing with Fire
Pleasure Bound
Red Hot Erotica
Slave to Love
Sudden Sex
Three-Way
Twisted

wrapped around your finger

a story of submission

by ALISON TYLER

CLEIS PRESS

Published in the United States by Cleis Press, Inc.,
2246 Sixth Street, Berkeley, California 94710.

Printed in the United States.
Cover design: Scott Idleman/Blink
Cover photograph: Emmanuelle Brisson
Text design: Frank Wiedemann

First Edition.
10 9 8 7 6 5 4 3 2 1

Trade paper ISBN: 978-1-62778-063-6
E-book ISBN: 978-1-62778-075-9

Sleep late, have fun, get wild, drink whiskey.
—Hunter S. Thompson

Introduction

Here I am. Ready or not.

I'm back with Jack and Alex—my man and *his* man. Or maybe I should say "both" of my men. Jack is my Dom. My Master. My lover. Alex is Jack's assistant: young, attractive, blond, and completely dedicated. Not to me. No, Sir—not yet, at least—but to Jack. I'm learning more about their relationship every day.

Or every night.

And I'm learning about who I am, what I'm made of. What I can give and what I can take.

Wrapped Around Your Finger is filled with pain and pleasure, with raw lust and the most base of human emotions—jealousy. The chapters in this book overflow with the needs you tell yourself in daylight are merely wants. But when the sun sets, when the urges build, when you can't help yourself any longer—those decadent wants become needs once more.

But let's get down to details. Let's read the stage notes and make sure every prop is in place. Because I want to draw you in, to put you right in the scene with us. I *need* you there, seeing what I see, feeling what I feel.

I left you in *The Delicious Torment* with Jack and Alex and me... I left you in a bedroom, on a king-sized mattress, in a topsy-turvy world where happily ever after could include two Mr. Rights.

Now, I want to draw you back into that room. If I shut my eyes tight I can still smell the whiskey from his glass. Watch the flames flicker in the candles. Hear the sound of his voice...

Listen hard.

I want you to hear him, too.

XXX,
Alison Tyler

Chapter One:
It's Raining, It's Pouring

Fade in with a snip. A memory. A highlight from yesterday. Fade in…

"You've known," he whispered next. "You have to have known. Alex's been with me for years. We're not…" he hesitated, rare for Jack, who always seemed to have the right words to say. "We're not exactly lovers." I knew he was being cautious because Alex was standing right there. "Not exactly. But…"

"But you have been," I guessed, and Jack said, "Yes."

Jack moved his body off mine, and he undid the cuffs. And then, while I watched, he snatched a shirt from his dresser drawer and handed the soft tee to me. I slipped on the shirt, swimming in the excess fabric, while Jack turned his attention to Alex. In moments, Alex was naked on the bed under Jack, Alex was being kissed and stroked and carefully attended to. Alex was being turned over, face-down on the mattress, while Jack lubed up his own cock with easy, thoughtful strokes. I sat on the chair against the wall, and I watched breathlessly as Jack fucked his assistant.

I wouldn't have left if the room had been on fire. I was mesmerized. Unwilling to move. Unable to think. I watched, the way Jack liked to watch me, watched as he bucked against Alex, as he gripped Alex's hips, as he rode the young blond with the smeared eyeliner and the ripe bottom lip.

"Can you deal with that? Can you live with that?"

I didn't close my eyes. I didn't turn away. I drank in every single second.

Once, at SFMOMA, I attended an unforgettable exhibit. A video screen was mounted on the floor in a small, darkened room, the screen facing up toward the ceiling. Displayed on the flat glass was an endless loop of people having sex—at least, that's what the film appeared to be. You could see the naked back of the person on top, and by peering down you received a voyeur's dream shot, watching the rocking motion, the rhythmic thrusting. The exhibit was the only item on display in the tiny space, and I never wanted to leave.

I wanted to stay and watch forever.

Could I live with what Jack was describing—or what I thought he was describing? Could I accept that Jack would never solely be mine?

In a way, that's how I felt this evening. Except, of course, I could see more. I could see the faces, the expression of total concentration in Jack's ocean eyes, the lust wash in waves over Alex. The echoes of desire. I could put myself easily into Alex's place, less easily into Jack's. I didn't try to categorize my feelings; I only watched.

Later, I would ask myself how I'd felt. Later, I would try to force my emotions into the correct box. A Pandora's box. An art-deco container labeled JEALOUSY. Or ENVY. Or DESIRE. But at the time, I was simply an audience member. It's not cheating if you all agree to the rules, right? Nobody's tearing a bond or breaking a promise. (*Keep telling yourself that*, I thought afterward. *Keep changing the rules to fit the scene.*)

I knew when Jack was going to climax. I knew because I'd seen that look on his face often enough when he was poised over me—or gazing at our reflections in a mirror. I saw the change in him. I saw him reach his peak, hold Alex's hips even tighter, and then freeze before bucking forward, as he came, forcefully came, ferociously came.

Alex let loose seconds after, panting hard as he shot, collapsing on the mattress in the tangle of rumpled, damp white sheets.

I stayed where I was, as if I had been cuffed there. As if I had been commanded by Jack not to move. I stayed and watched as Jack slid his fingers along Alex's fine muscled back, and then down his long torso, stroking him tenderly. And then I closed my eyes, as if I could feel the whisper of those fingertips on my own body. After several seconds—minutes?—Alex stood and headed down the hall to the shower. He seemed as dazed as I felt, lost in a world of our own creation. Jack wrapped the sheet around his naked body and leaned against the pillows. He didn't smoke anymore, but Alex did, and for some reason I wasn't at all surprised when he asked me to find him Alex's pack of cigarettes and the matches.

I watched him light up and blow silvery smoke rings to the ceiling.

I waited for him to tell me something. To say something. Anything. To explain the whole evening to me. Instead, he remained silent, smoking, eyes on an invisible point in the distance. Until finally, finally, he said, "Who did you think the toy was for?"

"Alex," I said automatically. I'd been sure I was destined to fuck Alex tonight. I would have bet money. And I would have lost.

"That's where your smart little writer's brain took you?"

"Yeah."

He rolled over and stubbed out the cigarette in his empty whiskey glass.

"Come over here," he said, and I climbed on the bed, sitting at his side, waiting. Still waiting.

"Lube yourself up."

Now, my heart was pounding as if I'd been the one recently pummeled. I got it. But I didn't get it. I understood. But I was lost in a haze of confusion.

"Use the lube and grease up your pretty cock."

At his request, I poured a handful of the clear liquid into my palm and jerked my fist on the toy, the way Jack had shown me. Not like a girl this time. Not like a girl at all. Then I watched, my whole body illuminated as Jack rolled over on the mattress and waited for me, waited for me to understand.

Chapter Two
Ashes and Diamonds

"You know what to do. What I want you to do." He wasn't looking at me. He wasn't looking at anything. "So what the *fuck* are you waiting for?"

The two of us were alone in the room. I knew fully how it felt to be taken like this. And I knew how it felt to *want* to be taken like this. To want and to be denied. My ex-fiancé, Byron, had refused so many of my desires, had tamped down so many of my needs. He had made me feel damaged beyond repair, disgusting and unwanted. I would not do that to Jack, would not turn on the man I loved. So I started to slide that lube-drenched toy between the fine cheeks of Jack's ass, and I felt hot tears streaking my face for no reason at all.

"Jesus fucking Christ, kid. What do you think I want from you? You think *this* is what I want?"

I was helpless. The tears blinded me. But my craving to please overpowered the fear. I didn't want to fail. Alex wouldn't have failed. But Alex was physically attached to his cock, and mine was synthetic and blue. Silly color choice. What the hell had I been thinking when I bought the device?

Jack was waiting, and I was letting him down.

His voice was sandpaper when he spoke again. He sounded distant, and yet I knew the power contained within the man right in front of me. "Don't make me ask again." The statement couldn't have been simpler or more impossible to ignore. The words were weighted with unspoken threats.

I conjured every bit of power left in me to thrust forward, to let him feel it—that's all he wanted. I understood. To feel it. He wanted to climb inside me, and there was no way for him to actually do this. He wanted to climb inside my body, to own every single part of me. To see what made my mind work. To feel the rush of the blood in my head.

And the blood *was* rushing.

I couldn't hear anything other than the sound of my own heartbeat. But I was fucking him. Oh yes, I was. And maybe I gleaned a bit about Jack when I did this. Maybe the voodoo worked both ways. It was almost as if I climbed into *his* skin for a moment, seeing my man submitting to me. Even if this was all a big act. Even if Jack could switch the game in a flicker, pull forward, take control. But he didn't.

"Harder now. Harder."

This was a display of trust that he let me continue, and I started to feel the pulse beating only in my cunt. Started to feel the wetness and the heat take over. My fingernails grazed Jack's skin, and then I pressed my body to his, my front to his back, and even while my hips were still rocking, I reached under him and touched his cock.

A light touch at first.

He groaned, his head down, and that sound took me to a higher level. I started to jerk him in my fist, no longer touching him tentatively or hesitantly. But touching him like he needed.

He said, "Jesus," again, but it was different this time. He said, "Jesus," and I knew that meant *don't stop*.

I was fucking him seriously, and he accepted everything. The pleasure from my palm and the sensation of being filled, and the whole fucked-up scene. He devoured it, somehow, from beneath. Until *I* was the one to let go. *I* was the one to come, that toy cock pressed so hard against my clit as I drilled him, the feeling of his rock-like rod in my fist. We were joined—we were one—and I came until I could hardly breathe, collapsed against him, liquid, spent.

Jack was in motion before I could think. He pulled forward, flipped me around, undid the harness like a pro, and discarded the tool. In seconds I found myself on my stomach. He didn't use lube. Trust me. He just fucked. Hard and fast. As if demolishing everything we'd done.

He fucked me like a machine, and when he came, the room seemed filled with the light you sometimes see through antique stained-glass windows: Shivers of light. Diamonds of light.

Or maybe that was only the look of the world through my tears.

Chapter Three
The Reason of Sleep

Jack brushed the tears away from my face and kissed me. He pulled the sheets and the covers up around us and held me in his arms until I fell asleep. In the morning, he was still there, not out for an early a.m. run on the gritty, glitter-dusted asphalt of Sunset Boulevard. Not off to work at his office. But right there, holding me.

When I stirred in his arms, he kissed me once more. Kissed my cheeks and my eyelids and my lips. I woke up slowly, warmth surrounding me, and I smiled when I saw him staring at me.

"Morning," I said, rubbing sleep from my eyes, blinking at the brightness in the room, the light letting me know how late I'd slept.

"Nearly afternoon," he countered.

"Where's Alex?"

And he told me. Alex had gone home during the night. Wherever home was. I didn't know if he and Jack had spoken after I fell asleep, but I thought that Jack hadn't moved. I felt that Jack had stayed with me. That he had made sure I was safe and cared for. That I was—in the most basic sense of the word—well.

I blinked and stretched, and I started to remember everything that had happened the night before. Jack was still watching me, fixedly, and I could tell he wanted me to say something. To comment in some way about the evening's events. Yet I had no idea what I was supposed to say. Did we need a postmortem? A footnote?

"Coffee?" he asked. I nodded quickly. Coffee always helps any situation, in my opinion. Jack slid into a pair of drawstring sweats and headed to the kitchen, while I settled back on the mattress and recalled the night. Was there a slick fragrant puddle of olive oil on the floor of the kitchen? Were the harness and blue cock hiding somewhere under the bed? Was the bond between Jack and me stronger than it had been, or had something been forever altered?

Jack returned quick enough for me to realize that he had been up while I'd slept. He hadn't spent all morning holding me. The coffee was already brewed, and he handed me a white porcelain mug, the type you find at '50s diners, and watched from the edge of the bed as I took my first few sips. I winced appreciatively as the strong, black liquid flowed through me. Now that I was more awake, I could look around the room and see that the whiskey glass with that lone cigarette stub was gone. My clothes—discarded at some point during the evening—were put away. Or thrown away? Set on fire? Everything was neatly back in its place. Everything but me.

Because I didn't know what my place was any longer.

"Feeling more alive now?"

I nodded. "More human. Yeah."

"Do you want to..."

I guessed that the next word was going to be "talk," and I shook my head. Jack's eyes went dark like rain clouds. "You a mind reader now?"

"No, Jack. I'm sorry."

"What did you think I was going to say?"

"Talk."

"Not 'go out to breakfast' or 'catch a movie' or 'fuck'?"

No, I hadn't. We rarely saw movies together, and I wasn't hungry in the slightest. But I was always ready to fuck, and Jack knew that.

"I don't want to talk is all," I managed to say. But that's what Jack made me do.

"Why not?"

Oh Christ. I felt as if I'd been shattered and needed time to heal. Every single part of me felt sore. I didn't know how long I would require to rebuild myself. Clearly, Jack was going to give me no time at all. "Because I don't have anything to say."

He nodded. "Fair enough. What if *I* have something to say, Princess? Do you feel like listening?"

I looked at him warily, but nodded. There was danger in his tone of voice.

"You worried that last night is going to become a daily event?"

Hell, no. That hadn't even occurred to me. What would that mean? Would I have a different set of harnesses and cocks for each night of the week? Red for Monday? Purple for Tuesday?

"Are you worried that I've changed?"

I shook my head once more. Jack hadn't changed. As far as I could tell, he'd simply peeled back a little more of himself for me to see. Revealed the inner workings, so that I could get a peek at what went on inside him. He knew almost everything there was to know about me. In comparison, I owned only a fraction of what made him who he was.

"Are you worried I can't take care of you the way you need?"

"No, Jack."

"Then what's the matter?"

"Nothing." If that was true, then why did I sound like a teenager who'd been told she couldn't use the family car? Sullen. Pouty.

Jack moved closer, smoothing my hair off my forehead, staring at me as if he could see inside of me. "Can you handle this?" he asked, not menacing, not challenging, almost as if he were curious. "Can you, Sam?"

He didn't rush me. He sat at my side as I sipped my coffee and thought about what that simple question encompassed. Could I handle being Jack's girlfriend if that meant he fucked Alex every so often? Or that he asked me to fuck him. Or that my whole world would feel occasionally as if it were upside down, as if I truly were Alice in Wonderland, falling topsy-turvy down the rabbit hole?

And then I thought about what it would mean NOT to be Jack's girlfriend. To be on my own. To be on that endless, sickening quest for someone who would understand me the way Jack understood me. Who wouldn't judge me. Who wouldn't be afraid of me.

I set the mug down. I turned and faced my man. I met his stare and held it. And I said, "Yes."

I meant yes. And then I found myself lost in a swirl of mounting insecurity. Jack was a bit like the devil, wasn't he? Giving me far too much information at once, too much sensory input, and then offering the contract to sign—in blood, of course—before I could gather my wits about me. In the safety of the bedroom that morning, in the glow of his blue eyes, I would have agreed to anything.

Pass me that razor blade. I'll make the cut. I'll dip my quill.

But as the day slipped past, as I found myself unable to write, unable to do much of anything but wander aimlessly from room to room, I wondered what I had actually agreed to. Were things different between us than they had been the day before? Or was everything the same: the same twisted, wicked, relationship that we'd managed to build together over several lust-filled months?

I didn't know. I couldn't tell.

Jack, true to form, was his usual self. Not as if nothing had happened, but as if everything had happened to his personal satisfaction. He spent the afternoon going over files from work, and the only difference at all was that I caught him smoking out on the balcony, seeming to savor the cigarette, lost in his thoughts. Jack had never smoked in front of me. Not until the night before. Did part of our agreement mean that all façades had crumbled? That everything was on the table now? Would more of his vices come into view?

My mind returned over and over to the images of the previous evening. When I entered the kitchen, I found myself lost in the feeling of being suspended once more, wrists hooked over the cabinet knob, while Alex reached for the olive oil. When I entered the bedroom, I saw Alex stripping down, or Alex dressing up, or Jack on his back, facing away from me, wanting...

"Yes," I said.

Alex was conspicuously absent, as if Jack had told him not to come by for the day, as if he'd said to make himself scarce, to give us time. I wondered where Alex fit in, still not convinced that the three of us could manage any semblance of an actual "relationship." How could we with Jack serving as Alex's boss and me cast in the role of Jack's sub? With Alex sometimes domming me, and sometimes ready to submit?

"Yes," I'd said. But what did *yes* really mean?

I thought about how I'd felt while buying the clothes for Alex, buying the sexy toys. I'd been titillated, that was true. And I'd been willing to go to this new place, to try being in charge for once. At Jack's instruction, that is. With Jack's blessings. But I'd believed the whole time that the night was to be dedicated to Alex, to his needs and cravings, and yet once more I'd been caught off guard by Jack.

That should have been no great surprise. Jack seemed determined to constantly push my boundaries, to make me do things I'd never thought I wanted to. Never thought I would. And then to prove to me that those very actions suited me perfectly. Like having me kiss the waiter in New York at his instruction—only to be punished for my very heartfelt obedience afterward. Or to be whipped by a stranger at a sex club, where everyone could see exactly what I was made of—pushed to a place where Jack had to take the pain himself. Or caged and hung overhead while Jack disciplined that luscious blonde Juliette. I'd been wetter than ever by being Jack's caged slave, yet tormented beyond belief by the view of him topping another female.

There was no reason to think that Jack didn't know what I was going through now. He was extremely intuitive. He was dangerously intelligent. Yet he left me alone all day, seemingly satisfied with simply being near me without needing to "check in," to "reconnect." At least, not until dinner.

* * *

He cooked for us that night. Cooked to a level that I'd had no idea he was capable of. He did so without any explanation, creating a beautiful array of savory dishes, like you see in gourmet magazines. He proudly served the meal in the living room, on the low table, each plate designed artfully. He sat on the sofa and I sat on the floor facing him on my knees, in proper position. Over dinner, Jack poured us wine—chilled white wine, because that's what I like best. And while he waited for me to appreciate the first sip, he said, "It's not a game, you know."

I looked at him and then set down my wineglass.

"This whole thing," he continued. "You. Me. Us. It's not a game. It's not normal, maybe. Not 'normal' the way most couples exist. But it is real."

Real. He was right about that. If I'd been unsure of my feelings toward Jack, the previous evening had definitely put things into perspective. I did not want to be without him. Yet I still didn't know how far I'd be able to go to be with him.

"I'm not stupid," he said. "I know this has been supremely difficult for you. And I don't pretend to have tried to make things easier by prepping you for any of my plans. That's not my style. Besides," he grinned at me. "I like to see how you act under pressure. I like watching you process new situations. You're a pleasure to observe. You spin things out so many different ways. You think so hard."

I listened to his speech, sensing somehow that this was leading to something new, something once again unexpected. What had he planned for tonight? Would his lovely personal secretary march in and make one of my naughtiest fantasies come true? Would Alex appear dressed in drag and act out the scenario I'd been certain would happen the night before? Or maybe there would be a trip to a sex club, or a dirty movie, or a back alley with me up against the bricks....

"It is real," Jack repeated. "You can feel that, can't you?"

I thought I understood. In the past, he'd occasionally paid for what he'd wanted—needed—and by paying, he'd gotten...well, he'd gotten what he'd paid for. Never knowing if the girl on the receiving end was actually into the scenes he prepared. Or whether she was simply after a tip. But what I did with him, what I was willing to do, the pain I yearned for, the level of humiliation I could accept, all of that matched his need to inflict the pain, to push down on the shame, to take me to the highs and lows that I craved. He was right. What we had *was* real. And who was I to think that everything between us would be fairy-tale perfect? Why wouldn't Jack's fantasies take different routes than my own? If we were connected tight enough on the deepest levels, then those twisting spirals of X-rated urges would ultimately all lead to the same happy ending.

Right?

"Like these are real," he finished, lifting his napkin and pushing an envelope across the table to me. I broke the seal, not having any idea what I might find within, but my hands shaking nonetheless. Inside were tickets. Tickets to Paris.

I'd traveled with my ex—but never abroad. I'd been to Europe with my parents. But that was different. I looked at the tickets—first class—and then back to Jack.

"I've been busy," he said, "I know that. But I can take a break right now, and I thought that we should..." He hesitated. "We should take a few weeks together."

If I hadn't survived the night before, would he have been handing me the prize behind curtain number one? Or would I be wherever no-man's-land Alex was? The thought appeared in my mind and then vanished.

He took the envelope from my hand and set it back on the table. "Of course," he said, and even though his voice had gone stern, there was a hint of humor in the tone. "I'll expect payment in advance."

"Of course," I repeated, feeling the excitement swell within me. Not only because of the impending trip. But because of the whole wild ride.

Chapter Four
Wonderful Tonight

"Eat," Jack said, looking at me as if he knew exactly the thoughts that were running through my head. As if he could see how ready I was to strip out of my clothes, to climb over his lap, to feel his hand connect with my bare ass.

"I can't," I told him. "I'm too excited."

His eyes flashed. "For Paris?"

"For everything."

When I saw the tickets, I felt faint. But when I heard the word *payment*, I got wet. Jack always insisted on being paid fairly, and although I had no idea what he had in mind this evening, I was desperate to find out. Still, I could guess—or hope—from prior experience, and I shifted on the floor, already eager.

Although I hadn't been abroad with a lover, I'd managed to enjoy two separate European romances. So I knew exactly how sexy the City of Light could be. Why else would Paris feature in so many of my short stories and erotic novels? Every chance my characters get they head to Paris.

"Eat," Jack said again, and I did my best, my mind thousands of miles away—waking up next to Jack in some fancy hotel. Drinking espressos at his side at a café on the Boulevard Saint-Germain. Shopping for frilly little nothings with Jack...

"There are some clubs I want to take you to," Jack said, breaking me from my daydreams. Or, rather, bringing fresh ones to the surface. "I'll help you pack so that you can be dressed appropriately. And I'm sure we'll buy you some new outfits there."

Outfits. That word conjured up brand-new visions by the second. Jack didn't mean sherbet-colored cashmere twinsets. When he said "outfits," he had costumes in mind. Fetish gear. Latex. Leather. Boots that buckled up the thighs.

I stared at my plate. How could I possibly take another bite? All I wanted to do was rush down the hallway and start packing. We had days before our departure, but I planned to spend every moment getting ready. Jack had other plans.

"Payment," he said again, forcing my focus back on him. "Payment starts tomorrow night."

"What do you mean?"

"I'm taking you to dinner with several of the partners. You'll have to be on your very best behavior."

I sat up straighter. Jack and I rarely socialized with the people he worked with. This was something new. "We're going to pass you around the table..." Jack continued. New and terrifying I should add.

I was already trained better than to say, "You're going to *what*?" But the words were in my head.

"I know you want to," Jack said. "I'm only going to make your deepest, darkest fantasies come true."

"What fantasies?" I had to ask. What did Jack think my fantasies were?

"We'll have the big back room at the restaurant," Jack said. "When we arrive, you'll strip down and get on your knees. I want you to service each man there."

"Service?"

"With your mouth, baby. With your mouth. I want you to suck them all until they're rock hard and ready. Your mouth is so sublime. I feel guilty that I've been so greedy with you. I should have been sharing this whole time. When the men experience that wet heat on their Johnsons, well. There's no saying what will happen. I'll have to take charge, to make sure they go slow. Then we'll really see what you're good for."

Was Jack fucking with me? I couldn't find my voice, couldn't figure out where to look. Jack's eyes were giving me no clear message. I sensed no level of teasing now. I stared down at the plate.

"And then?" I managed to ask, directing my query more to my food than to Jack.

"You want me to tell you everything, don't you?"

I nodded. I could feel the throb in my sex. My clit was swollen, my pussy sodden. I wouldn't have thought that those words would have turned me on so much. But Jack was spelling out desires I had never confronted in the past.

"We'll spread you out on the table, and we'll go to work. One man will eat your cunt while you suck another's cock. We'll get you so you don't know if you're coming or going. You won't know which way is up. By the end, Sam, you'll be this mess of longing, and we'll take you exactly where you need to go."

Where? I wanted to cry out. *Where do I need to go, Jack?*

"You'll have a man in your pussy, a man in your ass and one in your mouth. You can do that, can't you, Sam? You can take three at a time. I'm sure you can. Ultimately, you should be able to take more. A cock in each fist, perhaps. But tomorrow, there will only be three. You'd do that for me, wouldn't you?"

I didn't know how to respond. Was this one more of Jack's tests, the type that had no correct answer? If I said I'd do what he wanted, then I was as good as stamping the word HARLOT on my passport. If I declined, if I lied and said his story hadn't turned me on, then I'd be denying one of Jack's commands. Plus, all he'd have to do is touch me between my legs to know the truth.

"Look at you," Jack said lovingly. "You're a mess already."

I was trembling all over. Jack could get me into a state without much effort at all.

He leaned closer across the table. "You'd do it, wouldn't you? You'd do exactly what I said, Sam."

I would not look into his eyes. But I bobbed my head. Jack held my chin in one hand and forced me to meet his gaze. "Someday, I'll offer you a night like that. Someday, you'll be my little gang-bang whore. But tomorrow won't be that night."

Relief filled me. But the feeling was tinged with loss, as well. Jack had done what he'd said—he had named a dark fantasy. He had made his desire my own. If I wanted to now, I could call up this story any time. I could finish the plot, revise the scenario. Jack had opened a door.

"You'll do fine," he assured me, "I'm not worried

about that. But I'm sure the evening will be pretty dull. Still, it's time we went public."

We'd gone public. We'd fucked all over the town in public. He'd taken me in movie theaters. He'd done me against his car. He'd screwed me out at the beach. But I knew what he meant. After all, I'd been through a version of this before. Byron had kept our relationship fairly hush-hush until he was sure he was serious about me. Only then had he brought me to his mother and stepfather's country club brunches and to his father and stepmother's Saturday afternoon barbecues. Prepping me ahead of time about what was expected for each occasion. Giving me the rules of etiquette. Would Jack do the same thing?

"You'll be fine," he said again, and I wondered if he was trying to reassure himself or me. Was he nervous that I would talk porn with his cronies? That I would confess to the fact that I'd dropped out of the university three times and had no plans to complete my degree? Or was he afraid that his colleagues might judge him, judge him for dating a girl as young as I was, and as obviously unfinished? I knew the type of women the lawyers in his firm married. I'd taken their calls when I worked for Jody, the screenwriter in Beverly Hills, scheduling lunches, helping to organize benefits. They were ice queens. Holding fast at forty. Already nipped and waiting to be tucked.

And there I'd be at the table. Not so much waiting to be tucked—as waiting to be *fucked*. I actually smiled to myself as I thought that, and I managed to take a few bites of the meal Jack had so carefully prepared. That is, until he began speaking again.

"Tomorrow will be your first 'official' payment," Jack continued, "but we can put you on a prepayment program beginning tonight." He sipped his wine while he watched me hesitate, fork halfway to my mouth, waiting for him to finish.

"Start with a fashion show," he said, "of what you'd like to bring on the trip. You can gather up your favorite outfits"—there was that word again—"and I'll be the judge."

I couldn't finish the meal fast enough. I loved when Jack was in this sort of mood, positively playful, even if there was a visibly wicked look in his eyes. Yes, I was admittedly feeling nervous about the following evening, but I decided to deal with those worries in the morning. I'd had enough experience being around rich people, anyway. I'd interned for them. I'd served them in retail stores. I'd massaged their bodies and listened to their secrets. I could handle myself.

And now...now was fantasy time. While Jack took care of the dishes, I headed back to the bedroom to choose the lineup. I knew what I wanted to end with. But I had to plan accordingly. To stretch out the show. I grabbed handfuls of hangers from the closet and arranged my choices on the bed. I could hear Jack washing up in the kitchen, and I thought of how odd it was that he'd never cooked for me. Not like this. Not before. We'd had snacks and quick meals. Cheese and crackers. Champagne and grapes. But we almost always went out or ordered in. He seemed more relaxed tonight, I decided. More at ease.

That had to be because of the way the previous evening had unfolded, right? And the way that I'd reacted. Perhaps not the best I could have. But it seemed that I'd been accepting enough. Willing to try, at least. To learn.

As I chose the first outfit—a frisky French Maid costume complete with black fishnet stockings and an ultra-luxe feather duster (perfect for all of those hard-to-reach places)—I wondered where Alex was, and why he hadn't been by or called even once during the day. Could he truly be as satisfied with the events of the night before as Jack appeared to be? Was he off celebrating, or licking his wounds?

Jack hollered out to me, "I'm ready, Kid. What's taking so damn long?"

I slid into a pair of shiny patent-leather pumps and headed down the hall.

Chapter Five
Playing Dress-Up

"Oh, wonderful," Jack laughed when I emerged in my French Maid outfit. "You're here. Why don't you start with the bookshelf on that wall?" I shot him a glance, thinking that he would have wanted me to begin my work somewhere else...perhaps with me running the luscious feather duster along his bare chest, and then down, lower... I could so easily imagine how the tickling feathers would feel on his naked skin, and I wanted to make him shiver, to make him close his eyes as I ran the duster between his legs and over his fine, hard cock.

Or maybe he'd take the duster away from me and be the one to wield those unforgiving feathers. Maybe he'd tie me down and tickle me with the delicate feathery fronds. That was the only way I could conceive of being able to handle such torture.

But he simply raised his eyebrows and waited, seeming to want me to *actually* pretend to clean. In Jack's sterile world, dust never had a glimmer of a chance. His cleaning service was in every day to make sure of that. He liked his world beyond neat, bordering on antiseptic. But I began to whisk away the nonexistent particles, making sure to reach high up on my tiptoes and then bend way over to get into nooks and crannies while Jack sipped his after-dinner drink, watched me move in the tight, tawdry outfit, and gave me detailed instructions.

"Over here, Miss," Jack told me next. "I need a fresh drink."

"Yes, Sir."

I took his glass with a curtsy and refreshed the drink. Jack winked at me and then when I thought he might start to peel out of his clothes, he told me to head back to the bedroom. To try something else. He really *did* seem to want a fashion show. A naughty, fetish-filled fashion show, but a fashion show, nonetheless.

The bed was covered with possibilities. But as Jack had given me zero indication of what would turn him on this evening, I had no idea which outfit to slide on next. After some thought, I settled on a sexy secretary look, one with a crisp white collar attached to no shirt at all, a jacket open to reveal a sultry black-lace bra, and the shortest pencil skirt in the history of skirts. I kept on the fishnets, and then picked up one of my notebooks and a pencil. I knew that Jack's secretary didn't dress in any version of this clichéd style at all. She shopped in tony Beverly Hills boutiques, and sported a professional look—a look that I personally would never, ever want to adopt. But this was different. This was a secretary outfit made from vinyl. Notebook in hand, I headed back down the hall.

Jack was on the balcony, watching the lights. "About time," he said, when I walked out to join him. "I did have a little dictation I wanted to get through tonight."

I stood, my pencil poised and ready, but Jack removed the implements from my hand. "Not that kind of dictation," he continued, pressing down on my shoulders. I dropped easily to my knees as Jack undid his slacks, and as I started to suck him, I thought about the fact that he rarely ever wanted a straight blow job. There was always an extra bit of kink thrown in—we were outside, or I was dressed up, or I was tied down, or I was crying from an over-the-knee spanking, trying to keep my ass in the air. Jack twisted the perverted dial on every scene, which was exactly what I desired.

Taking "dictation," in this manner felt as if Jack had decided to tap into that particularly shameful fantasy I had of attempting to be his office secretary, but failing in every way. Failing, at least, except in *this* way, my mouth hungry and open, Jack's hard cock teasing past my lips and down my throat. He started slowly, clearly in no rush this evening, and I worked him to the best of my abilities, tricking my tongue around the head of his cock, sliding it down the shaft. I remembered all of the lessons I'd learned. I relaxed my throat. I protected him from my teeth. I even hummed a little bit, so that he could feel the vibrations.

Jack stroked my short hair as I sucked him, and then, as I fell into a rhythm, as I felt we were working together, Jack said, "Oh, Danielle, just like that, exactly like that," and I almost choked.

Danielle was one of the perky, front-desk receptionists at Jack's office. I don't know why I hadn't seen that coming, or why the effect was so great. At my hesitation, Jack sped up, now forcing his cock at the rhythm of his own choosing, making me breathless, bringing tears sparking to my eyes.

"What's wrong with you today?" he crooned. "Usually, you're so good at this, Dani. I'm surprised at you."

All I could see was the pretty blonde. She'd been polite to me the few times I'd talked to her, the random occasions I'd met her, but I hated the vision of her bent on her knees in Jack's office, hated it enough that I couldn't keep up with Jack. He clutched me by my hair and pulled my head back, demanding with his actions that I look up at him.

"No good," he said, "I'll have to send you around to the other partners, so that you can get a bit more practice in. I could feel teeth that time..."

Then back he drove, slamming his cock all the way to the hilt, so that my eyes watered further with the power behind each thrust of his hips and my mascara began to run down my cheeks. Again and again he thrust into me, and I did my best to regain my control, my ability to please him, but I felt as if I were drowning. Failing. Floundering. Jack had taken control so easily. He had shown me who was boss with only a few casual remarks. Then he stopped, and without cracking a smile, he put his hands under my arms and jerked me up to my feet, sending me back down the hall for outfit number three.

My face was wet, and I stood in front of the mirror and looked at myself. I was slightly disheveled even though Jack had hardly manhandled me at all. The evening was taking a different direction now. Not so lighthearted, but sexy regardless. I used a tissue to wipe away the black smudges of mascara. I quickly retouched my makeup and then considered the remaining outfits in a different frame of mind. No, I didn't think Jack was actually accepting blow jobs from his staff, but the image was fresh and raw in my mind, and what had started out as a fairly friendly fashion show had now become more intense.

Dress-up with Jack was always an event. He made sure that we possessed a range of interesting attire, a veritable treasure box of outfits destined to spur the libido. If Jack felt like playing a sadistic cop intent on fucking an escaped con, I had the black-and-white striped Lycra prisoner's dress to go with it—and he had the cuffs and the nightstick. Oh, that nightstick.

What might he do if I wore the naughty nurse outfit? How might he react to the cowgirl or the pretty plumber, or the cheerleader, or the superhero? Who can deny a girl in a cat mask?

I looked back at my number-one outfit, the only thing in the mix that I would actually wear out of the house from time to time, the one that made me wet, the one I had been holding out for last. And then I said to myself—fuck it, I didn't feel like being a genie or a fairy or a frightened wood nymph. I cut to the chase, sliding into the plaid schoolgirl skirt, choosing a pair of day-of-the-week panties, tying a knot in the white shirt so that my flat midriff was exposed. I put on cherry-red high-heeled Mary Janes, started back down the hall, and then stopped. Inspired.

Where had Jack gotten the cigarette last night?

From Alex's pack.

And where had that pack disappeared to when Jack had cleaned up the room?

I looked around the bedroom, then rifled through one of Jack's drawers, locating a nearly empty pack and a golden lighter tucked under his socks. Feeling a delicious wave of anticipation flare through me, I lit the cigarette, replaced the lighter, and headed down the hall.

Chapter Six
Light My Fire

I never smoked.

Even when my best friends got stoned in a neighbor's hot tub, I was the one who brought the snacks and laughed at their antics, but I never smoked. My high school beau Brock favored Marlboros, and I remember watching the silver wisps curl toward the ceiling of his bedroom—that was after I stopped being a good girl, obviously—but I never reached to snag my own cigarette from his pack. I can't even imagine what his response would have been if I'd tried. A hand slap? A spanking? A lesson, for sure.

In college, one of the students illegally smoked Kools in her dorm room, and she would light me one and try to teach me to inhale French-style, but I would let the thing burn down while I listened to her tell stories. Not that I think smoking is cool—I'm just saying, I had no experience. This was a prop in every sense of the term.

But Jack thought it was something more. Jack thought I was fucking with him. Because he'd never smoked in front of me before, because clearly he only lit up in cases of stress beyond stress. The only thing I knew Jack was enslaved to was his physique. He ran, he worked out daily; there was no way he smoked regularly. So when he saw me with that cigarette in hand he took the symbol to mean that I was messing with him.

At least, that's how he acted.

"Where did you get that?"

First words out of his lips.

I didn't even try to inhale. "Found it."

He laughed darkly, a 180-degree flip of the laugh he'd given me when I'd appeared as a French Maid. This was his don't-lie-to-me laugh. I'd been hoping for some "Daddy's gonna teach you not to smoke" scene, and what I'd walked into was, "Daddy's gonna teach you not to go through his drawers," which was something different entirely, let me tell you.

"Give me that."

I walked forward, so meek already, the cocky attitude disappearing in a breath. I handed over the cigarette and watched as Jack walked to the balcony and stubbed it out. I was already trembling. The events of this evening kept catching me off balance. I felt as if I didn't know where I was, what I was doing.

"Now tell me," Jack said, returning to the living room and sitting down on the sofa, so that I was standing in front of him like the naughty fucking schoolgirl I was dressed as. "What was going through your twisted mind when you grabbed that pack?"

"I thought..." I started.

"No," he interrupted, "you weren't thinking. If you'd been thinking, you wouldn't have opened the drawer."

"I mean," I said, feeling the flush of heat creeping up

my jaw. "I was trying to find something else. Something extra for the outfit."

He nodded, as if he understood, but his face had that look I couldn't read. Was he playing with me or was he actually upset? I could never tell. Didn't matter though. The results would be the same.

What *had* I been thinking? That he would slide into the role of teacher or parent or principal or headmaster, catching his schoolgirl smoking after class. That he would punish me to remind me not to do so in the future. Punish me as he saw fit. But now we were talking about something else. I'd gone through his belongings without permission. Why hadn't that occurred to me as I'd pushed my way under Jack's socks, as I'd held the gold lighter? A solid lighter, one that indicated that perhaps he wasn't a regular smoker now, but he had been at one point. Had someone given the lighter to Jack as a gift? Was the relic special? Was that why his cruel Dom eyes were regarding me so seriously?

"Bend over the table," he said now. The coffee table was low, and I had to kneel in order to obey, but I did so immediately, supremely grateful not to have to be looking at him anymore. His eyes were scaring me. That wasn't a comforting feeling.

Jack didn't move, and I didn't speak. Time played with my head. I knew he was staring at me. I could feel his gaze on me. But I kept my face down, aware of the fear running through my body and the arousal building by the second. I would not fail again. I would wait, no matter how long he took, for his next instruction.

Finally, Jack stood, and relief made me sigh. Relief that didn't actually materialize. I'd thought he would unbuckle his belt, but Jack headed to the bedroom instead. I heard his footsteps, heard the sound of his cabinet opening, but kept my head down. I would behave, I told myself. In spite of being dressed as the most insolent schoolgirl of all time.

I would make Jack proud.

When Jack returned, I didn't look up to see what implement he'd chosen. I kept my eyes lowered, trying to show him with my attitude that I was learning, that I was submissive and humble and...

Jack would have none of that. "Kiss it," he said, brandishing the paddle in front of me.

Jack had chosen the one with the studs, and I had to muster pure courage to raise up and press my glossy lips to the hateful thing. I remembered when he'd brought this one home. "The salesgirl said it wasn't for beginners," he'd told me, "but I explained that you could take pain like nobody's business." He'd clearly relished the fact that he'd been able to discuss his punishment sessions with a stranger. But I'd been that much more embarrassed the next time he took me shopping at that particular store with him, wondering which salesgirl had flirted with him, which one now knew I was regularly paddled at home.

"What are you being spanked for?" Jack asked next, and my shoulders sagged. I wanted him to simply spank me. I hated lectures or being asked to name my sins. I understood that this was why Jack insisted on this part of the scene. Still, I didn't even try to get away with, "Because I was smoking." We both knew I'd gone way beyond that lie.

"I went through your drawers."

"Yes, you did."

"I shouldn't have done that without your permission."

"Right again," Jack said.

"I'm sorry, Jack." I actually glanced up at him this

time, and he gave me a little half smile, as if he couldn't help himself. I must have looked so fucking pathetic.

"No," he said, as I'd known he would. It was almost a ritual between us, the words he said next. "No, you're not sorry. Not yet. But you will be."

He started by spanking me against the plaid pleated skirt. The pain was muffled, and Jack knew this. I think he was giving me a moment to gather my thoughts, to steal my emotions.

He raised my skirt after only a few blows, smacking the paddle on top of my panties. I always managed to forget how much this particular paddle could hurt. I drew in my breath, trying to find a way to deal with the sensation, but Jack was working too quickly. Slapping the paddle repeatedly from one cheek to the other, then covering both with the full length of the mean thing. I white-knuckled the edge of the table to keep myself steady. I didn't want to make a mistake and try to cover my already smarting ass with my hands, didn't want to irk Jack any more than I already had unintentionally. I didn't even want to think about what would happen if I failed again.

Would he stand me in the corner with my ass on display?

Would he make me bend over while he fitted me with one of the largest of our butt plugs?

Would he wash my mouth with soap?

Tears started almost instantly. Tears of shock, I think, at first, and then from the true pain. Between spankings, my mind plays tricks on me. I tell myself I can handle anything. That I am an elevated being. That pain means nothing to me. And yet, as soon as I am in the proper position, as soon as I hear the whistle of the paddle cut through the air, I'm done for. Lost. Another bad girl getting spanked to tears. Look at me now, boys. Look at me now.

He didn't make me count, which was a kindness on his part. He simply paddled me, mercilessly, until I found that I was holding my breath between strokes, my whole body tense, only breathing to gasp at the intense pain wrought by those demented studs.

But I couldn't help myself—I wondered. Would he be satisfied with leaving my panties on tonight? I started to believe that maybe Jack had a little pity left in him, and that was exactly when he told me to stand up and head to the bedroom. My legs were shaky. My whole face was flushed and tears had left my cheeks salty and shiny.

I could feel Jack watching me walk to the bedroom, and I tried to envision what he would do to me when I got there. Would he strip me naked, or keep me in the costume? Would he make me take down my panties, or would he tear them off himself, his fingers yanking the cotton down my thighs?

Somehow I had the feeling that no matter what happened tonight, we would not be done with this scene. That what I'd unwrapped would come back in the future. If not to haunt me, precisely, then to strike me once more.

Chapter Seven
Temptation

"Go on. Get."

The walk to the bedroom felt like miles. Jack was behind me, and I knew better than to drag my feet, to slow things down. Yet I wasn't about to sprint ahead, either. How strange that I crave being spanked the way some women crave a sexy kiss or a subtle caress or an unexpected deep red rose wrapped in tissue, and yet at the moment of—or the moments before—the punishment, my mind always races for a way to avoid the inevitable. The thought of the pain gives me pleasure when I fantasize hours before—or hours after.

The actual event nearly robs me of my nerve.

Jack waited for me to open the door, to walk inside, and then, because he'd given no instruction, he watched as I found myself backed into the far corner. I hadn't headed to the bed, or to the chair. I had nowhere else to go.

"I started smoking in high school," he said, surprising me. I'd expected, "Take off your skirt and bend over the bed." Or "Pull down your panties and then turn around and touch your toes." Or any one of the many ways Jack instructed me prior to a bottom-blistering spanking. Instead, I watched as Jack opened the top drawer of his dresser and pulled out the lighter. "And would you believe, this was a gift from my father on graduation." He smiled in an odd way as he rolled the lighter in his hand, obviously appreciating the weight of the device. "He smoked, too, and you know, I think he liked the fact that I was taking after him. Something men did. I quit after college, but every once in a while, I still desire the experience." He laughed in a relaxed way, a confessional way, so unlike Jack I felt unnerved. "You know, I adored everything about smoking. The accessories, the way it felt to have a cigarette in my hand. The ashtrays from faraway places and the foreign cigarettes I'd buy abroad. I liked smoking in bars, playing pool or drinking and shooting the shit. I was a smoker's smoker."

Jack rarely talked like this. Showing off some sort of weakness. Or not weakness, but a soft side.

He shrugged. "I kicked the habit for all the reasons that people usually do. Health. Fear. But I still hold on to that lighter. And every so often, I don't know, once or twice a year, I'll snag a pack from Alex and smoke until they're gone."

Why was he telling me all this? I couldn't fathom.

"Seeing you with that cigarette let me know you went through my drawer," Jack said, and I got the feeling we were reaching the end of the story, the last stop on the line. "And I know you don't snoop. I know you better than you probably know yourself. You want to find out things about me."

I opened my mouth to say something—who knows

what—but Jack didn't hesitate long enough for me to get myself into more trouble.

"Don't kick yourself for that. Any normal girlfriend would. But you've been supremely self-controlled in that aspect. I've even tested you. I'm not sure you're aware of this fact. But I've left out clues, tricks, and you've passed each one…until now."

"I wasn't…" I started weakly, feeling the heat in my cheeks again. I'd been lost in the vision of Jack in high school. What he must have been like. Some tough kid, right? Smoking behind the gym. Some rebel. Except, he couldn't have been too rebellious in order to get into the university and law school he'd attended. He must have been a mix, a blend, the way I'd been. A smart kid with a leather-wearing rebel's desires. But now, we were back, and we were in the moment, and I was damned.

"Doesn't matter the reason, really," Jack said, still observing me in that casual, almost scientific way. Sizing me up. "You did what you did, and you'll be punished for it." (Oh, my pussy clenched at those words. Still clenches, to tell the truth.) "But you can rely on the fact, Sam. I will tell you the things I want to when I feel the time is right. I'm a private person. Extraordinarily so. Maybe pathologically so. You know that by now. Yet I have shown you more of myself than I've ever revealed to a girl before."

"But," I tried again, "I wasn't snooping Jack. I wasn't. I was just looking for…"

"Doesn't matter," he said once more. "This is more of a preemptive punishment. Something for you to remember in the future, if you're ever tempted. You can understand that, can't you?" He smiled again, warmth lighting his features. "In fact, you *like* that." He seemed to lick the edges of those words as he spoke them. "This is the sort of punishment that resonates within you. So that later, you can think back, replay each and every moment when you're in bed after I've gone to work. When you're stroking yourself." He caught the embarrassed look in my eye and he continued darkly. "Trust me," he said, "I *do* know you better than you know yourself. Don't think you can hide things from me."

Why was I so careful with Jack? Why did I never look in places that I had been barred from? Why did I avert my gaze, force my hands to remain at my sides? Simple, really. I was a reformed snoop. In *The Delicious Torment* I told you about the poem I read that Byron had created for me, but never shared with me. What I didn't tell you was that I knew he'd bought the engagement ring months before he handed it over. I had a feeling he was hiding something, and I went on a search that I'm sure so many women can relate to, locating the ring in a shoebox on the top of his closet. And after that, there was just the waiting between us until he popped the question one evening. Not even a special or important date. One he felt was right. (It was wrong. All wrong.) But the months when I'd known he had it, when he still treated me poorly, or like someone would treat a moronic member of a household staff, that was what had ultimately turned my heart to glass. How could he treat me like that when he wanted to marry me? That's what I never could comprehend.

So for Jack to think that I had snooped—intentionally, anyway—that made me sick inside.

But not as sick as seeing Jack reach for the cane.

Chapter Eight
How Do You Make a Sadist?

One part whiskey
Two packs of Marlboro Red
Pinch of gunpowder

There's no one recipe. But as soon as Jack brought up his father, a person I'd never even thought to imagine for some reason, I wondered whether there had been some sort of odd relationship between the two. Was Jack ignored as a kid, and that's why he'd grown up to revel in this life of dealing out pain, or trading pain for pleasure? Or was he like me, fundamentally hardwired to want what I want—or, more truly, the reverse of what I want—from the start?

The can was opened for me, now. I wanted to know what his life was like. Life before me. I wanted to know everything. Why hadn't I wondered before? Why hadn't I played those invasive little girlish games? On quiet evenings, couldn't I have curled up next to him on the sofa and asked him pointed questions, drawing him out as the level in his whiskey bottle grew lower? I might have pumped his cock in my fist and dipped down to lick the head while he grew more talkative, in between sighs and moans.

The truth is simple. The reason I'd been so patient is because I've been decimated in the past. Most often in my life, when I've found out someone's secret, I've realized I actually was happier without knowing. Take my first true love: Brock. I'd assumed he was on the level with me. Why? Because I'd never met a criminal before, let alone dated one. So when his devious life came pouring out in a soul-crushing rush—well, hell, I wished I hadn't opened that door. Wished I'd never searched. Wished he could have kept everything sinister away from me and saved me from the truth. The harsh realities of the world.

But this was different.

I was with Jack. And I felt that there was nothing I wouldn't tell him about myself. Nothing he couldn't ask, that I would not willingly reveal. So why was he taking so long to bring me into his confidence? Why had he played out that scene with Alex for so many nights? Why couldn't he sit me down and lay out all the facts?

Now was not the time to ask, surely. Not when Jack had his favorite cane in hand, when he was instructing me precisely how he wanted me on the bed. When the look in his eyes had hardened, turning from that pure blue to solid ice.

"Take off your top."

I did so quickly.

"And your shoes and stockings."

I hurried to obey, all the while feeling Jack's eyes on me, admiring me, drinking me in.

"I'm not going to cuff you," he said, and my heart

sank. I'm not sure how it is for other submissives out there in the BDSM universe, but for me, it's always so much easier to be bound. When there's no chance of escape. No choice but to accept every bit of the pain in store. Being bound tight is freeing, as odd as that sounds. To have cuffs in place, to have leather straps on my ankles, to be forced into one position—how can I possibly find that easier than to behave in the manner that Jack said: "You're going to have to do this yourself, find the strength from within."

God, this night was odd. There was more give and take with him, more discussion than usual. More revelation. And, as I might have expected...more pain.

I assumed the position on the bed. I felt Jack undo the schoolgirl skirt and slide the tiny rectangle of fabric off my body. I arched my hips so he could slip my panties all the way down and off, and then I shuddered. Unable to help myself, to stay still. I shuddered as if the room had dropped ten degrees in temperature. As if I were outside in a snowstorm, the flakes sticking fast before melting on my naked skin.

How do you make a sadist?

Jack didn't speak. Instead, he watched me while he moved back and forth around the bed. He played with the cane, tracing the tip along my spine, then down between the split of my asscheeks. I remained still, as still as possible as those silent shivers worked through me. And then, to add to my discomfort, that incredulous voice in my brain started chiding me:

Why are you doing this?

Why are you with someone who is about to hurt you, to mark you?

Why the fuck would you need that?

And then the other voice, the one connected directly to my desperate cunt, responded:

Oh, god, why doesn't he start?

Why doesn't he let the cane connect?

Why is he making you wait so fucking long?

He was an expert. Oh, yes, he was. Jack was my sweet sadist with an iron will. He knew perfectly well what agony I was in before he even brought the cane down once. A well-practiced sub can punish herself (or himself) with thoughts alone. A die-hard sub can dive into that place where the pain will be pleasure from the very first stroke. And Jack waited until I was there, until the only real pain for me would have been if he'd dropped the cane and left the room. True pain would have been no contact at all, the misery of solitude, of being alone with my perverted longings.

I made no sound as the first stroke perfectly landed precisely across both of my cheeks. I tensed, because I had to, because I had no other choice, and a different type of tremor worked through me. Grateful, I was, that he had begun. Satisfied, I was, that he had taken pity on me. At least, in his fashion.

He struck again, a bit lower, catching the meatiest part of my ass, the fullest part. I squeezed my eyes shut, squeezed my thighs together, and thought, *I'm going to come.*

How could he have gotten me there so quickly?

His silence. His sharing. His secrets. I was a whirlwind of confusion. Of curiosity. I was a mess, a hot mess, as Jack struck again, moving quicker now, yet with purpose. Slicing into me with finesse. I kept my arms locked over my head, in the manner he'd requested, in the style he'd required, fingers laced together to help me keep from failing. I didn't thrash. I didn't move. I accepted each blow, swallowed up the pain with my bottomless need, and waited, helpless, for him to strike again.

In flashes of understanding, I saw my hand on the dresser knob, pulling the drawer open. Had I known this would be the result? Had I pushed Jack on purpose, even subconsciously? Or was this night about something else, something entirely different?

The force he used rocked me from the inside, and when Jack paused after ten blows to slip his fingers between my thighs, he laughed out loud. My pussy betrayed me. This was no punishment. I was wetter than ever, wetter than I could have anticipated.

"Good girl," Jack said, losing the cane to the floor and then stripping off his own clothes. "You stayed still for me, and I know that wasn't easy. That couldn't have been easy. I didn't hold back." He was behind me then, sliding his cock in my wetness. He fucked me so that I felt exactly how turned on I was, and yet how bruised, as well. His body slammed into mine. There was nothing soft now. Nothing remotely tender.

Because Jack knew what I know in my soul: tender doesn't work for me. Tender makes me crazy. I needed the full fierce fucking that Jack gave me. I needed him to absolve me and fill me and make me his pet once more.

"You can come," Jack said, and to back up his words, he rubbed his fingertips over my clit, dialing my number with those decadent rotations. "Come for me, doll," he whispered, pressing a little harder as he sensed my body's desire.

I fell into the pleasure, let the sensations crash over me. Jack raked his short nails down my skin and I contracted again and again on him as the climax stretched out, fresh vibrations rushing through me as if the pleasure would never cease. When he came, he arched forward and bit the flesh on my shoulder blade, leaving marks I knew would last for days.

Marks I wished would last forever.

Chapter Nine
Punish Me with Kisses

Sex with Jack was brutally passionate in every possible way. When we fucked, I felt not only physically used, but mentally demolished as well. Afterward, I didn't only want to sleep, I wanted to put myself back together. Not so much like Humpty Dumpty, with eggshell-fine skin. But like a one-thousand-piece jigsaw puzzle that's been scattered around the room, some colorful pieces raining like confetti down onto Sunset Boulevard, never to be seen again.

Jack understood.

He knew that I lived for the feeling of being wrecked. I was an art history major with a seriously skewed sense of beauty. The most attractive I've ever felt has been on mornings after I've been up all night. Makeup smeared, lipstick all but kissed off so that only a scarlet stain remains, eyes open by sheer will and the blessed power of caffeine alone. I strive for that look sometimes intentionally. I don't bother with my hair, simply wrap it around my fist until the wayward curls knot upon themselves. I choose aubergine-hued eye shadow palettes. Standing in front of the vanity, I slide on the crimson gloss and then wipe away nearly every trace so that the bathroom cabinet is littered with tissues covered in lipstick kisses.

But that night was different. That night, Jack didn't fuck me, bite me, hurt me, and then roll off and go to sleep. Instead, he did what I'd wished from the start, what he'd denied me at the beginning. He cuffed me, used leather bindings on my ankles and chrome-and-leather cuffs on my wrists. He made sure I was stretched out on the mattress, made sure that the room was warm, and then he discarded the crisp sheets and cashmere blankets and brought his body next to mine, his fingers stroking me. Gently. Softly. Putting me back together himself—not forcing me to do the serious mental work on my own.

He was kind to me in those early morning hours. His fingertips lingered long and slow on all the bruised places. (Once upon a time, I wrote a story called "The Madness in the Middle" about the intense pain that comes from pushing on a bruise, and the strange craving a submissive always has to do exactly that.)

The night should have gone by slowly. As slow as Jack's fingertips retracing every place the cane had landed. Every mark he'd left. But when I think back, those hours passed in a blur. Colors fading quickly behind my shut lids. I was tense at first. Thinking he was prepping me for something else, something new, exotic, and dangerous. He didn't talk to me, he didn't tell me what was going to happen next. He didn't warn or chide or cajole. He simply touched me, his strong warm hands finding all the right places or all the wrong places.

All the places that hurt.

I've confessed the unusual fact that I was a masseuse who despised being on the receiving end of massages. Strange beast, yes, but it's the truth. Thankfully, Jack wasn't rubbing and soothing. He was tracing, as if trying to understand the marks on the surface and the pain that ran deep inside of me, the connection between the two. He made me hurt more, with that gentle touch, and he made me cry, for no reason at all. Until I felt that we were brand new. That he was discovering me for the very first time.

Does that make any sense?

I felt as undeniably connected to him as I had out on the balcony a million years before, when he'd put me outside naked. When he'd whispered to me not to worry so much about my own deviant desires. That he needed the same things himself.

This night, this quickly passing night, set me as off balance as I had been when Jack pushed me outdoors and shut the glass door. I was left teetering by the silken caresses of his fingers. I was left unsure and confused as he touched each place with his own flesh, places that had been burned by the brutal bamboo of his cane. I was lost and I was found.

Without a word from Jack.

Jack didn't bind me for the caning, but he bound me for the featherlight touches that came after. The part that would generally have made me flee; the part that some women, other women, desire. He bound me so that he could stroke my body in a way that he wanted to, a way that would usually have been abhorrent to me. Too soft. Too pure. Too different.

Give me metal. Give me bitter. Give me gravel and neon. Give me broken glass and jagged edges. A nasty smirk. A rough aside. I don't know what to do with the candy-fluff, with pastels, with rose-scented sweetness.

Jack traced the lines and welts left by his cane, the bruises left by his paddle. And then, as the day broke, he brought one of the blankets off the floor, wrapped his strong arms around my still-captured body, and let us fall slowly—finally—to sleep.

Chapter Ten
Coming Out

In the morning, Jack was gone. I've always considered myself a light sleeper—and I guess I was in the past. The past before Jack. But after those sorts of nights with my Dom, I slept hard. Hard enough not to wake when he uncuffed and unbound me. Hard enough not to realize that I was alone in the bed until the sun's rays woke me.

Jack had left me a note about how to dress for the evening's dinner. *Dinner.* I'd all but forgotten that this was my "coming out" party. Jack was planning on parading me in front of his coworkers, and he wanted me to make a proper impression. He hadn't said that, precisely, but from the note, I understood.

Nothing slutty. Nothing too young. Nothing that he would normally approve of, request, or fuck me in.

I wrote for a while—the morning was all but gone—and then I called my friend Elizabeth and begged for an emergency appointment at her salon. I still wasn't accustomed to fixing my hair in this short, pixie style. I knew how to make myself look like a punk Kewpie doll, with rhinestone-studded clips strewn throughout, but that wasn't what I was striving for this evening. As I'd known he would, Elizabeth's best friend did an astounding job, making me appear professional and sleek. He left me with a highly polished look, which was my goal.

"What are you going to tell them that you do?" Liz asked me afterward.

"Write."

"They'll want to know what you write. People always want to know. They'll ask if you write screenplays or pilots. If you want to be the next big thing." She spoke these words as if I were dumb not to have guessed this myself.

I knew that Liz was both mildly horrified and endlessly intrigued by the genre I'd chosen. And at the moment, I'd landed a new gig, reviewing sex toys for a national magazine. Every time I visited her, I brought bags of toys to share. Mostly ones geared for men, that I knew Jack would find too bizarre, but which the hairstylists found good for a laugh. The thought of Jack taking a penis enhancer seriously was a joke to me.

"I'll lie," I said.

"But you're going to see these people over and over," she insisted, pulling me out back to the patio, so that she could smoke her beloved clove cigarettes. "You're going to have to remember what you say, what you tell them. Otherwise they'll catch you up at the next cocktail party, and you'll embarrass yourself and maybe Jack."

I thought about that, and I wondered why my man hadn't prepped me for this important portion of the evening. He'd been concerned about my attire, but not about my attitude. I considered calling him at work, but I hated to interrupt him. He was supremely focused when at the office, and I didn't want to intrude.

"Tell them you write romances," Liz suggested, adding her fragrant smoke to the smog of L.A.'s sky. "That's not really a lie."

"What if someone wants to read one?"

"Say you're still working on trying to get published."

"Maybe I'll tell them I'm in school."

"That's no good. Jack will look like he's dating young."

"He *is* dating young."

"You know what I mean. If he's asking you to meet his cronies, then he's letting you—and them—know how important you are to him. If you say you're a student, you'll be making him look as if he trolls the playground for dates." She gave me a sharp look. "Don't you go wearing one of your slutty schoolgirl skirts!"

"I wasn't going to," I promised her, and I wished once more that Jack had given me extra information. Maybe there'd be time to talk before we went to dinner.

Back at home, I searched through the closet, seeking the most sophisticated outfit I owned. First, I tried an emerald cashmere dress I'd bought in Paris after graduating from high school. The above-the-knee number was formfitting, and I always wore it with a wide black leather belt (chic at the time) and deep-purple cowboy boots. Although I had won plenty of compliments for the outfit, I shook my head at my reflection. Next up was a pants suit I'd bought for a holiday party—muted red velvet, too tight to wear with a shirt beneath, lots of skin in a deep *V.* Wrong, wrong, wrong for this event.

After careful consideration, I landed on a selection I'd often chosen when conducting interviews while working for the newspaper. I categorized this as an outfit Audrey

Hepburn might have worn had she worked on a paper. Yet I still managed to make the pencil skirt and crisp white blouse look as if it were part of a costume. A sexy librarian costume. The cut of the skirt was the slightest bit too tight to be professional, the shirt too fitted. My stack-heeled spectators added to the pinup effect.

Jack had said not to dress sexy.

What the fuck did that mean?

Everything in my closet screamed sex, but at least this wasn't low-cut. Wasn't too short. Wasn't dyed a deep crimson or shimmery black, cut from expensive butter-soft leather or glossy PVC.

I did my makeup carefully, which took twice as long as usual, and then I paced. I hadn't written for the full amount of time I normally did, but I couldn't even think to go to my notes. Do actresses act on Oscar days? The thought of trying to squeeze out a few extra paragraphs made my head ache. Instead, I strode to the balcony, then back to the mirror, waiting for Jack. Hoping he'd like what he saw when he entered the apartment.

Jack arrived home late; a conference call had gone longer than he'd expected. He hurried to change for dinner, giving me only the most cursory glance on his way to a fresh shirt and jacket. At his request, I poured him a drink and brought the glass to him, then sat on the edge of the bed to watch him change.

I loved watching Jack get dressed. Unlike me, clothes never looked costume-y on him, only correct, as if everything had been cut for his body. He wore sweaters that fit him divinely, jackets that emphasized the broadness of his shoulders, the sleekness of his physique. Watching him dress relaxed me. I snuck a sip of his whiskey when he set the glass down, meeting his eyes in the mirror and catching him winking at me.

"You're scared?"

Easy for him to guess this. My discarded outfits were still draped on the chair near the closet.

"Nervous," I admitted.

"Anything I can do to help?"

I tensed automatically, an animal in the wild sensing danger, ears pricked, eyes narrowed. Jack was being unexpectedly solicitous, and I had not yet seen him since our erotic encounter the evening before.

"Liz said they're going to ask me what I do."

"And what are you planning on saying?"

"That I'm a writer?" I hated the question mark at the end of this sentence. I'd had one book come out from a well-respected publishing house, had several more in the pipeline. I was a writer with an exclamation point by now, wasn't I? A writer! "Is that a problem?" I asked Jack.

He shook his head. "I'm not ashamed in the slightest of what you do," he said. "You tell them whatever you're most comfortable with. My guess is that they won't talk a hell of a lot to you, which I'll apologize in advance for. Most of these guys don't know how not to talk shop."

"And the wives?"

"You're familiar with the type already."

I nodded, feeling more nervous than ever. Yeah, I knew the type.

"Back to you," Jack said, dressed now, his drink almost finished. "Let's figure out what we could do before we leave that will help take your mind off your nerves."

I shut my eyes. I lowered my head. I waited for him to continue. Knowing, somehow—or guessing, rather—what Jack might suggest.

Chapter Eleven
All I've Got Tonight

"Stand up straight. Look at me."

I bit my lip. I was scared—scared of trying to behave correctly around his work contacts. Scared of being labeled a little kid again. Someone inconsequential, or even laughable. The women in Jack's social circle were unbelievably wealthy. They shopped at places I didn't dare enter. Places where nylons cost three hundred dollars. If I had stockings like that, I'd leave them in my drawer and stroke them with my fingertips but never dare slide them on. (I squirreled away enough money once to buy myself a sheer Gaultier shirt. I couldn't bear taking the beautiful item out of my drawer.)

There was no way for me to actually fit in. The night was all going to be a fake.

And I knew about nights like this.

During my years with Byron, I spent many uncomfortable evenings with his friends. He had a way of collecting people who were as pompous as he was. They would spend endless hours around a table at a diner or lingering over some high-end dinner, spouting unbelievably idiotic comments about whatever play, movie, or concert we'd seen. The fact that the whole group would be stoned only made their observations that much more interesting to them and that much more dreary to me.

Now, I was being set up for an evening with lawyers. Lawyers and their wives. It wasn't that I'd had my fill. I simply wondered why I'd never ended up with a man whose social circle intersected my own, or even slightly overlapped mine. But while I could coast through encounters with Byron's inebriated buddies, this was going to be different. These people were smart and focused, as driven as Jack, and unlikely to be giddy from good Hawaiian Gold.

But Jack was offering me salvation.

Not in the form of a bong hit, or a quick shot of tequila. He knew that wasn't what I craved.

"Let me see you," he said. I stood up even straighter, shoulders back, head high. For the first time since he'd arrived home, he took the time to look at me. The blouse. The skirt. The hair. The shoes. His expression softened in approval—I knew I'd done what he asked. Then he said, "Let me really see you." I met his blue eyes, unzipped the skirt, and stepped out of the garment, showing off the garters and stockings beneath, turning around for Jack, because I understood precisely what he was asking.

"Take them off, baby."

I slid the panties down and stepped out of them, now wearing only the crisp white shirt, stockings, and lovely heels. My favorite black-and-white heels.

I couldn't see Jack's face, didn't know what he was

thinking. But he came forward, his warm, strong hand caressing my naked curves, his palm running over the welts from the previous night's caning. I wondered what he would do next. What I wanted him to do. My pussy hummed to life, as if he'd flicked on a motor inside me. From his words, I'd understood his offer. He was going to give me something to take my mind off my nerves. And the miracle cure offered by Jack would always include pain or humiliation.

"Bend over the bed," he instructed, and I obeyed, growing wetter by the second.

Jack pushed me farther up on the mattress, and without any warning he started to lick my pussy from behind, pressing his face against me, getting deep into me. I groaned and spread my legs as wide as I could, trying to find the best position for him. Jack always knew how to touch me. The way he worked—his tongue, his teeth—brought me almost unbelievable pleasure. Do you think I write oral in a sensual manner? Thank Jack.

He made tight circles around my clit with the tip of his tongue, and I sighed and arched, wondering how far he'd let me go. But this time, he only allowed me a quick taste before he moved, now parting the cheeks of my ass and licking me there, so that I was wrecked, my pussy spasming over and over at the sinuous intrusion of his tongue. I did my best to stay still, but my whole body was rocked with the decadence of the experience. He kept up, making those dreamy circles with tongue, his hands splitting me open like ripe fruit as he tongue-fucked my ass. I thrashed on the bed, not caring that I was rumpling my once pristine shirt, that I was ruining my carefully coiffed hair. Not caring about anything except Jack's magic tongue.

He was rough with me, his hands pinching my still-tender skin, taking breaks from licking around my hole to bite me, to nip at the raspberry-pink stripes decorating my ass. And then back he'd go, licking, thrusting, one hand sliding under my body to pinch my clit in a rhythm that had me on the verge in seconds. Or kept me on the verge.

This was good. This was better than I'd dared imagine. I loved when Jack got into this type of mood, because he became insatiable, wanting me to come from this sensation alone. He loved to lick my ass as if he were eating my pussy, and I was embarrassed by how much this treat turned me on. He turned his head back and forth, tickling me with his short hair. He licked my hole over and over with the flat of his tongue before spearing me with one finger, then two, corkscrewing the digits to finger-fuck my tight back door.

Then he was up, rummaging for something in the cabinet and returning again, too quick for me to think of what he was doing, too quick for me to stop the protest as I felt him wet me with lube and then start to slide a plug between my cheeks.

"No."

"What did you say?"

Cringing away from him, from the word, from everything, I pulled a few feet upward on the bed before he could manage to get the plug inside. How could I? How could he? My mind reeled. I realized that Jack honestly wanted me to sit at dinner with a toy inside of me. What was he thinking? I'd be ruined even by a smallish one like the plug he'd chosen. How did he expect me to converse with his friends, associates—whatever the fuck they were—with a butt plug nestled in my ass?

"No, please, Jack."

He laughed, and I knew I was lost. He laughed, and I

realized he'd planned this from the very start. Made me get myself all ready, all pretty, all fluffed up, only to knock me down off my pedestal once more. Show me how he really liked me. Show me what he really wanted. I was broken. I was in pieces. He hadn't let me come yet, either, so my body reverberated with hopeful longing.

"Did you say *no*?"

Had I?

I felt trapped, pinned down like a butterfly on a corkboard, my delicate wings fluttering uselessly, stirring the sex-perfumed air. There was nowhere for me to go.

"If you know what's good for you," Jack continued, his voice only slightly more serious, "then you will roll back over like the sweet girl I know you are and spread yourself wide apart for me."

I wasn't a good girl. He was mocking me. And what he was asking for wasn't good either. I had no time to decide, to check my options. I looked at him, into his eyes, and I sighed and resumed the position, reaching back, parting my cheeks for Jack's pleasure. I was wet everywhere, and he slid the plug in easily—so easily, I was mortified by my body's response. Then he stood me up and reached for my panties, holding them so that I could step back in.

"I think you'll need a different shirt," he observed wryly, and I saw that in my thrashing on the bed, I'd managed to smear crimson lipstick all down one of my sleeves. "And I'd advise a quick retouch of your makeup."

I glanced in the mirror over the dresser and saw that I had one of my most treasured looks in place. A love letter to Robert Smith from the Cure, Tim Curry from *Rocky Horror,* but nothing I wanted to sport out to the exclusive restaurant in Hollywood. I could only imagine the looks on the wives' faces when they saw me walk in.

Tramp.

Trash.

Trollop.

Trembling, still, I got back into my skirt, then stood in front of the closet and chose a different top, a formfitting, fine black cashmere crewneck sweater and matching cardigan—a vintage '50s twinset. Jack watched me adjust my outfit, gave me a pat as I walked past him to the bathroom to redo my makeup. There was no fixing my hair, though. I couldn't recreate the sleek look the stylist had given me. So I resorted to my standard spikiness, sticking a few rhinestone clips throughout. My attitude had definitely been adjusted. So what if I looked younger than the nipped and tucked wives? I *was* younger. So what if I had a punkish persona? I couldn't compete with the women in their world.

But they couldn't compete with me in mine.

Was that Jack's lesson of the evening?

I had no idea.

He came in as I was finishing, and I left him alone while he washed his face and brushed his teeth. I was in the living room when he emerged, ready to go, smiling at me to let me know that there was more.

"Expect a three-hour meal," he said. "It always lasts at least that long. Can't get around that. It's why I don't socialize with these people that often."

I nodded.

"And expect me to fuck you afterward."

I nodded again.

"All right, beautiful," he put out a hand to me. "Let's go..."

Chapter Twelve
Ice Queens

"Jack! Good to see you! And this must be..."

"Samantha."

I wish I could say that the evening was easy. That my fears were unwarranted. That the couples we dined with offered nothing but warmth and companionship like in one of those old retro black-and-white movies where people talk fast, drink gimlets and compliment each other on their fashionable attire.

I could say all of those things—but I'd be lying.

We met the three other couples, who were already well into their drinks, thirty minutes after we were supposed to arrive. The restaurant was of the cold, sterile school of thought. Clean lines. Sharp edges. The waitstaff seemed to have been hired for their cheekbones and angular jawlines. There was nothing cozy or homey in the place. The framed, stark photographs on the wall were disconcerting, scary even. The floral arrangements appeared fragmented and sharp. Bird-of-paradise buds with their beaks still sealed shut. I was grateful for my sweater. The temperature in the main room was chilly, and I thought perhaps hell wouldn't be hot after all. Because this place came close to my definition of the underworld.

Jack didn't seem to care that we were late. In fact, I found his entire attitude rather odd. He'd made such an intense production of the fact that I needed to behave well for his coworkers. And then he turned my world upside down, leaving me barely able to walk in a straight line, my whole body humming with unfulfilled pleasure. My ass stuffed full with the rubber plug. Another one of Jack's dangerously sexy Dom tricks.

As soon as we sat down—with me trying not to noticeably squirm in my chair—Jack ordered us drinks, and then did the briefest of introductions. He spoke so quickly that I barely heard—and promptly forgot—each of the other diner's names. But it didn't matter. I was rarely addressed directly.

The men dove into work conversations, something I actually was accustomed to, having been around Byron's father and brothers on enough occasions. But the women were something else. Exactly what I expected?

No, sweetheart, they were far worse.

These were the girls I'd avoided in high school. The popular crew of tall, tanned, and shimmery goddesses who looked good in lipsticks with names like Salmon Ice. (Who came up with that winner?) They were members of the look-but-don't-touch crowd. So blonde. So fair. Thin enough to be practically transparent. Their manicures were perfect and tasteful. No sky-blue polish for them. Nude or oyster with a subtle gleam on their fingertips. The rocks on their rings were designed to speak volumes, diamonds so big I imagined the jewels weighed their little bird hands down. Maybe this was why they were so skinny. Perhaps the heavy jewels on their fingers made eating difficult. I lifted my drink too often to compensate for the fact that nobody was talking to me, and then felt Jack's eyes on me when the waiter asked moments later if I was ready for another.

I nodded. What the fuck, right? You only die once.

I wish I could say that I was bold and brave. That I jumped into the conversations with witty observations like a treasured comic sidekick. (Where were my leggings? Where was my cape?) But I'd be lying. I felt like I always did around people this rich, as if I should be working for them, not dining with them.

Not one of the three women at the table had a job. These ladies talked only about fundraising, plastic surgery, and fashion. Of the three topics on the table, fashion was the only one I could relate to—but my style did not compute in their world, as was obvious by the incredulous looks they gave my thrift-store cardigan. These women wore outfits that were chic but understated, nothing that would linger in your mind long enough to describe.

I wish I could say that I was well behaved.

But I'd be lying.

By drink number three, I didn't really care. I was quiet and I sat up straight, and I looked as if I were paying attention to the conversations swirling around me. Anyone who's spent time daydreaming in class knows how to fake this attitude. In reality? I was mentally writing X-rated stories featuring the wives fucking the waiters, the husbands fucking each other, taking turns giving and getting blow jobs. I recreated Jack's fantasy gang-bang story from the previous evening, imaging what would happen if I threw caution to the wind and spilled that tale to the wives.

Can you imagine? Sometimes in situations this uncomfortable I worry that I might cross a line. That I might really do something like lean in and say, "My boyfriend suggested that I become the fuck toy for the night. He told me he was going to rent the room in the back and pass me around to your husbands like some sexual appetizer. Each one would have a turn at me. Licking my pussy. Fucking my asshole. Or licking my asshole and fucking my pussy. Would that bother you? Would that be a problem?"

But I sipped my drink, and I bit my tongue, until finally, something happened that didn't just break the ice, it broke the cubes into tiny, powdered crystals.

One of the blondes had gone off to the ladies' room, and apparently had attempted to phone her long-distance lover, only to discover that her calling card had been canceled. (Yes, Virginia, these were the days of pay phones, which seems so charmingly vintage now, but definitely put a crimp in a love affair at the time.) She stormed back to the table in an absolute white-hot fury, and launched an unbelievable tirade at her husband. (Clearly, I hadn't been the only one drinking heavily.)

The husband appeared more shocked than the rest of us. And as the events of the evening unfolded, it turned out that the wife had:

a) dialed wrong—her husband hadn't canceled her calling card;

b) outed the fact that she was cheating on her spouse;

c) given her man a very good reason to divorce her and put an end to her lavish lifestyle.

Suddenly, I found myself far more interested in the people around me. When the couple took their heated discussion outside (never returning to the table), the two other wives actually began to include me in the gossipy conversation that followed.

"I *knew* she was still seeing him," one said.

"They never broke up. She played him when Dave thought she was playing tennis."

Jack and the remaining two men seemed mildly stunned by the commotion, although not as intrigued as we women were. The boys simply resumed their talk of work one man short, while we girls dissected what facets of information we had been given. Our end of the table became almost like a slumber party, with whispered confessions and drunken questions.

"Have you ever cheated?" from one wife, in a hushed tone, "I mean, before you were with Michael."

A shrug from the other wife, and then all eyes focused on me.

"Yeah," I said, my voice hoarse from lack of use.

"But it's different when you're only dating," this from the thinnest, blondest wife. The one I was sure had been head cheerleader when she was in high school. The one who would have been perched triumphantly on the tippy top of the people pyramid.

"I was engaged, though," I added, as if that gave me street cred, and the women wanted to know more. I felt Jack watching me, felt him paying attention even if there was no way he could hear what I was saying. The restaurant was known for its poor acoustics. There was always a dull roar in the background.

"Why'd you do it?"

I comprehended their world, these ladies. I knew that one of my massage clients had engaged in a long-term relationship with a man nearly identical to her husband in every way except for the fact that he paid attention to her.

Her husband gave her everything she could desire except his attention. Her lover called her "baby." She told me that he seemed to see her, whereas she'd become just another belonging to her husband. Confessions pour out so easily when you are naked and under a white sheet. Probably easier than in a shrink's office. But these women, pulling their chairs closer to me, eyes lit up, they were looking for something else in my words. They were looking for the excitement lacking in their lives of fundraising, Pilates, and shopping. At least, that's how it seemed.

"I don't know," I said. But that was one more lie. "I strayed because someone else said I was pretty." Oh, he did. He said I was pretty, and he said he couldn't wait to be inside me, and he stroked my hair and he kissed my lips, and he let me feel his hard-on in his black Levi's...

The thinnest wife cut her eyes at me, as if that was the lamest excuse she'd ever heard, but the other gave me a sympathetic look as if she understood.

"But how about the sex?" the friendlier wife asked me. "Was the sex amazing?"

Oh god, yes, I wanted to say. Yes, it was. It was everything sex is supposed to be. It was exactly what I'd always hoped for and then some. And if you don't believe me, check in with Connor. He's living in Georgia, chasing his dream.

But before I could say anything, Jack was at my side, sitting in the chair vacated by the cheating spouse. We were past main courses now—thank you, lord—ready to order dessert, and he seemed able to pull away from the conversation of men and join the ladies' end. His appearance changed the atmosphere, and the women sat back, sipping their drinks, talking once more about dresses they were ordering from Neiman's for various events. I was accustomed to that world, too, from the point of view of the help.

"If you don't mind," Jack said, "I'm going to borrow Sam for a minute." He didn't wait for their response. He didn't need their approval. He pulled my chair back in his gentlemanly fashion, and then he led me to the corridor leading to the pay phone and the restrooms.

"Enough excitement for one night?" he wanted to know.

"The last part sort of made up for the first part."

"And what about the *next* part?" he asked, watching as one of the unisex bathrooms opened up, ushering me forward and stepping into the room after me. The square room was designed in the same style as the rest of the chic location: Black tile on the walls. A urinal and a toilet. Black paper towels in a modern dispenser. A single ebony rose in a silver vase.

"This part?" I asked.

He gave me a nod, watching as I lifted my skirt for him, as I slid my panties down. "Your stockings, too," he instructed, and I gave him a blank look, while he folded his arms and waited. Carefully, I stepped out of my shoes, unhooked the garters, and pulled off one stocking, then the other. This old-fashioned action never failed to arouse me, the homage to a style from yesterday. Jack took the fine hosiery from me, and in moments, he'd bound my wrists behind my back with one of the stockings, the knots so tight, I couldn't move my arms at all.

He pressed me up against the polished black-tiled wall, and then reached between the cheeks of my ass to pull the plug out, leaving me feeling empty and open, forgetting where we were, forgetting the duo of ice queens remaining at the table, the men in their cookie-cutter suits. The odd-flavored sorbets melting in the dishes.

"Are you ready?"

"Yes, Jack."

"Then say it."

"I'm ready for you, Jack."

"Tell me you want it."

"Fuck me, Jack. Please, I need you inside of me..."

"Say it again. Keep saying the words."

"Fuck me, Jack." It was as if I were biting off the hard consonants between my teeth. Chewing on the words. Gnawing at them. "Fuck me, Jack."

He did precisely that. On the mantra I was whispering, Jack thrust hard, his cock driving into my pussy. I *was* wet and ready, and I felt lit up at how hard he worked me, illuminated even more brightly when he continued to talk.

"You know where I'm going to take you next."

"Yes, Jack."

"Say it."

"You're going to fuck my asshole." My pussy swam with sex juices as I said the statement out loud.

"I've been like a rock all through dinner, thinking about this. Thinking about what I wanted to do with you. I couldn't wait any longer. You drive me crazy. Do you understand that?"

"Yes, Jack."

"Watching you with those dead-eyed corpses. You're so alive compared to them."

He'd seemed immersed in work every time I looked his way, but now it was clear that he'd been keeping an eye on me throughout the endless nightmare of dinner.

"And I thought about you, with that toy in your ass, trying to act normal. Trying to behave like a good girl. Trying your best to blend in with the beige ladies."

I had been. He'd noticed.

"But you can't blend in, Sam. You're not like them. You'll never be like them. Thank fucking god."

He pulled on the stocking as he fucked me, slamming me forward, yanking me back. And then he was out, and I knew what he wanted, felt him bending me, but I couldn't help him. Couldn't put my hands forward to keep myself steady. I had to trust him, to know that he wouldn't let me fall. He'd never let me fall.

Jack gripped me with one hand and worked his cock between my cheeks with the other, until he was inside me once more, inside my ass this time, fucking exactly as hard, as ferociously.

But now he gave me another peek into his psyche. "If you ever cheated on me," he said, and I knew he was thinking about the scene at the table, merging that drama with what he knew about my past, with what he knew I was capable of. "If you ever..."

"I wouldn't, Jack, I won't."

"No, I know," he said, his voice harsh, so that I could tell he was close to coming. I was panting, so close, too, every part of my body electrified by his touch. Desperate for the way he moved me, the way he molded me. I was tipsy from the drinks, but felt fully aware of every single sensation. Awakened. On fire. Jack made sure I reached my climax first, using the heel of his palm to cradle my pussy, giving me the pressure I needed, the force to grind against. And grind I did. I spread my legs apart and let him hold me up with his palm, so that my juices made his hand all slippery.

When he came a beat after, he rocked into me so hard that I moaned, louder than I'd expected, the sound echoing off the tiled walls. Anyone close enough to hear would have understood what that noise meant. There's no way to hide the sound of a perfect O. I was a girl transported. Then I heard the stocking tear as Jack pulled the knots free, and I realized once more where we were, and what we'd done, and...

"Leave the stockings," Jack said, observing me as I patted myself with tissues and then stepped back into my panties. I pulled my skirt down, feeling the wetness slick between my legs, the dampness remaining. I stepped barefoot back into the heels, understanding that I had to go back to the table. I had to face the women. And they'd know. They'd know what we did. They'd tell themselves that this was why Jack was with me. Someone too young for him. Too short. Too not-blonde. Not like them at all. They'd judge me and dismiss me so that I wasn't a threat at all.

Jack grinned at me. "And you know what?" he crooned, pulling me into his arms and then flipping me around, so that I could see our joined reflection in the bathroom mirror. "They can think whatever they want, jealous witches. I don't give a fuck." He faced me once more, so that he was looking directly into my eyes. "You get that, don't you?"

I nodded and repeated my two most-used words for the evening, "Yes, Jack."

He led me from the bathroom, stockings and sex toy discarded in the metal wastebasket by the sink...something for the next patron to drop paper towels on, and wonder about.

Chapter Thirteen
Seven Days

I had a week to get ready for our trip. Jack warned me ahead of time that he would be busier than usual, and Alex was still conspicuously absent from our cocoon. But I had learned my smoking-hot lesson. Jack would share when he wanted to, when he was in the mood. I would wait, a well-trained (and well-pampered) pet, for him to parcel out bits of information like decadent treats.

At least, that's what I told myself:

Wait.

Don't push him.

Don't ask too many questions.

But waiting was difficult. I was jumpy, excited, wanting to talk with Jack all the time, to ask him which outfits he thought I ought to bring. I would have spent every evening with him, discussing our trip, sharing with him places I hoped we could go. Museums and stores, galleries, restaurants, out-of-the-way parks, hip secondhand stores.

"Of course," Jack said, about anything and everything. “Yes, whatever you want. I need to read this and get back to Michael before nine.” His mind was on his work. I knew that I should retreat to the office and write. But I tried and failed. I’ve never been able to be Zen about anything. I can’t calm down when I’m worked up, can’t slow down when things seem to move too fast. Which is how I got into trouble. If I could have given Jack space, if I could have done what he asked, the week would have passed smoothly.

Instead…

“Should I bring this?” I asked, with a twirl to show off one of my most treasured outfits, white sundress with spaghetti straps over a sheer blue T-shirt. Thigh-high stockings. Docs. I’d been packing for hours. Packing and repacking. Wanting to take my entire closet. Wanting to reinvent myself in Europe and be someone else. That’s how it always is for me when I prepare to travel. Bring what I love? Sure. But better yet—bring what that other me would love. Jack had bought me a collar, which I only wore to clubs. What if I wore that out every day? Would they let us into five-star restaurants in Paris? What if I brought a leash?

“Yes,” Jack said, not even looking up. “Yes.” Then, “Come on, Sam. Please. I’ve got to finish this.”

Jack rarely worked this intensely at home. He generally stayed late at the office if there was something pressing, dedicating his evenings to me. So I felt shunned, brushed aside. And because this was Paris we were planning for, Paris where we were going in only seven days, I couldn’t still myself. I couldn’t retreat with a glass of wine to the bedroom to read. I couldn’t go out to the bookstore down the street and buy foreign fashion magazines.

I had to bother Jack.

"What about this?" was my next query, pushing his limits, pushing the levels of taste, to be perfectly honest. I was now in a pair of buttery-soft scarlet leather pants and a long-sleeved cream-colored shirt, which should have been worn over a camisole or at least a bra, but which I had on over my bare skin so that my breasts were visible through the thin fabric. "Could I wear this?" I was trying to get a rise out of him, and unfortunately—or fortunately depending on how you look at the situation—it worked.

Jack set down his papers, and I read the expression on his face. If my fairy godmother had appeared and granted me one solitary wish, I wouldn't have gone for money or fame or world fucking peace. I would have taken back the last interruption. I'd pushed him too far.

"Listen," he said, his voice low and even. "I have to call Michael and go over these notes. And then, little filly, I'm going to spank that ass of yours until it's as red as those leather pants." His tone didn't change as he continued his speech. "And every night this week, after I'm finished with work, I am going to spank that ass of yours, just as firmly and as seriously as I'm going to tonight. You can count on it. When you wake up in the morning, the first thing you'll think about is the way I'm going to punish you each and every day."

And then he went to make the call, dismissing me while I stood in the living room. Not sure what to do. Where to go. What to say. He'd tell me in moments, I knew. He'd explain exactly how he wanted me. Exactly how to proceed. But for now, I was even twitchier than I had been before. Pressing him for attention, fighting to be noticed. Why had I done this? Why hadn't I been patient and behaved for Jack? Because that's not my nature. Being good never has gotten me what I desire.

I forced myself to sit on the sofa, lifting his near-empty glass and draining the last few sharp drops of whiskey. I crossed my legs, then uncrossed them. Was this what I'd been after the whole time?

I shut my eyes. I've never been easy with lack of attention. Byron was the king at ignoring me, and I always responded in this same way—by begging with my actions for him to notice me. The results weren't the same, obviously. Byron never lifted a hand toward me, never took off his belt in a way that made my stomach drop and pussy grow wet. But being ignored felt the same. Is that why I'd acted like this for Jack? Falling into some old familiar routine? Or was I simply so damn excited that I couldn't control myself?

Didn't matter, did it? I could try to decipher the rationale behind my behavior, or I could fantasize about what Jack was going to do when he got off the phone. As might be expected, I chose the latter. There was no way he'd let me keep on those choice leather slacks. That was for certain. The material was well tanned and thin, but would offer far too much protection to my haughty ass. Would he spank me here, in the living room, or maybe out on the patio, or...

"Get in the bedroom." Jack had returned before I'd had time to fully prepare. I hurried to obey his command, nearly tripping over myself. Jack followed behind me, slowly, and I was waiting for him, seated on the edge of the bed and nervous as all hell, when he arrived.

"I was planning on taking things easy on you this week," he said, his words almost sounding like a confession. "But I guess you need something else. Some sort of proof of my affection." His eyes glowed. "So while I was walking down the hall, I developed a plan." My heart—

oh, my heart—was pounding at his words. "Tonight, Sam, we'll start a seven-day regimen. Strip down and put on your white nightgown." He stayed in the room, watching me peel out of the leather pants and lose the creamy blouse, then rummage for the nightie he was talking about, antique white, voluminous, like something from the early 1900s.

"Over my lap," he said, and I hurried to his side, draping myself into proper position, then waiting, still, while he slowly lifted the nightgown, revealing my naked skin.

His hand was all he used this night. Firm, hard, unyielding. His hand was all he needed to make me press down on his lap, trying to gain contact with my clit on his knee. His hand was all it took to show me that he hadn't forgotten about me, hadn't chosen to disregard my constant yearning for his attention.

Jack's hand made me cry.

And then, when he was done warming my ass for me, his hand made me come, parting my thighs so that his fingertips could slap directly against my primed pussy. He found the right rhythm from the start. He punished me and pleasured me in the same way, a spanking on my ass and a spanking on my cunt. Jack never held back when punishing my sex, which was something that further linked me to him. He knew exactly how hard I could take—how desperate I was for him to strike me here. He wasn't afraid of me, or of my desires. That's what sealed us together so strongly.

The first part of the evening's erotic equation made me cry out, and the second part made me climax, Jack using his four fingers together, taking me the way I wanted, taking me over the top. He didn't give me permission to come, but he didn't tell me not to either. So I sighed and tossed my head, my body filled up to overflowing with the pleasure that he brought me.

"Admire yourself," Jack said, and I knew what he meant, what he wanted. I traipsed over to the mirror and I turned around and lifted my nightgown to my hips. Over my shoulder, I looked to see that my asscheeks were all ablaze, Jack's handprints easy to discern in places. He'd made my skin so rosy red. I blushed as he must have known I would, admiring his handiwork, delighting in my twisted way at the vision he'd left behind.

"You like that," Jack said, and I nodded and then caught myself. "Yes," I told him. "Always." He motioned for me to come back to him, and I let the nightie flutter into place as I crossed the room to his side.

"Seven days," he whispered as he pulled me into an embrace on his lap, my naked bottom smarting against his slacks. "And you know what, baby? I'm going to enjoy watching you try to find a comfortable position on the plane."

Chapter Fourteen
Worrying, Wondering, Anticipating

"A seven-day regimen." That's what he'd promised me. Seven days of spanking. The perfect gift for a sub who has everything her heart could possibly desire.

The next day was a mixture of heaven and hell. All day long I knew I was in for a spanking. All day long, this was the one thing I could think about. Craving and dread warred within me to such a degree that I was almost useless to perform even the most pedestrian task. Not that I had anything truly important to do. I was fully packed by now. My latest projects were finished. I didn't have any regular place to be, any clock to punch, any pressing deadlines.

Which left me with plenty of time to think about seven days of spankings. One every night when he got home from work.

Why was this any different from our normal life? Good question. Jack spanked me often—in many places in our house, and around the greater Los Angeles area. (Did you see a black-haired minx getting her bottom warmed back in the day? That was probably me.) The difference was that generally, I had no idea what to expect from my man, no idea what Jack might be in the mood for. Would he cuff me, blindfold me, take me somewhere outdoors to fuck? Would he bring me to a club or escort me to a sex toy store where I could watch, mortification flaring through me, as he hefted the various items of his current pleasure—and my future pain.

This was different. He might as well have penned in a spanking for each day on the calendar. It was all I could think about:

How long would he make me wait?

What toy or tool might he use on me this night?

Would he give me a teasing sort of pre-sex spanking?

Would he go for the long haul, pushing me past mere tears to actual sobs?

I must have come four times during the day, retreating to the tub and the delirious pulsing rain of the faucet, then to the bed, and my own knowledgeable fingers, and then to our array of toys, choosing a trusty vibrator. I spread my legs; I arched my back; I closed my eyes and replayed visions of our most decadent scenes together. The ones that had made me climax in real life. The ones I continued to screen in my mind whenever I needed a fantasy.

Jack was going to spank me.

He'd spelled it out. He'd told me so. I loved him for that fact, and I feared him for the same reason. He had to know what his promise had done—or truly, *was doing* to me. He had to know that I would be completely consumed by the worrying, wondering, anticipating.

And he did.

In the early afternoon, Jack called me from his office.

"You writing, Sam?"

"No," I said honestly. There was no reason for me to lie and tell him I had been productive. He'd have seen through the fib even over the phone. What if he asked me to read him what I'd created? Where would I be then?

"Packing?" he queried next, and there was humor in his voice.

"Uh-uh."

"Sliding those naughty fingers of yours between your nether lips and touching yourself?"

"Yes, Jack."

"And thinking of what?"

"You know." As soon as I spoke the words, I realized that had not been the correct answer.

"You're already getting *one* spanking tonight," Jack said somberly. "Are you trying to go for two?"

"No, Jack," I stood up straighter, even though he couldn't see my improved posture, and I forced myself to pay more careful attention to Jack's questions and my own responses.

"So tell me," my man continued, "what are you thinking of?"

"You spanking me." It was fact. Total fact. And yet, as always, the words were difficult to say. You ought to see me at public readings. How pink my cheeks get when I reach the dirty parts of a story. Yes, I am the shy pornographer. I always have a tough time with the X-rated words. Not writing them, as you can see. I can write *cock* and *pussy* and *asshole* like the best of them. But there are certain terms and phrases that give me pause every time I have to put a voice behind the words.

"So tell me," Jack repeated. "Tell me what you're thinking."

I pressed my legs together. Jack's request was so damn sexy, and yet what he was asking me to do was so damn hard. And he knew it. All I wanted was for him to drive home right then and take care of this need of mine. Yet I dreaded that moment just the same. It's what makes wanting a spanking so conflicting. Never changes. At least, this sensation has never changed for me, even after all these years in subspace. I approach every spanking the same fucking way. With embarrassment. With excitement. With lust. And with some variation of heart-pounding fear.

"What am I using on you in your dirty little fantasies?" Jack prompted me, and I guessed he had his hand on his cock.

"Your belt," I said immediately. "The one you wore today. You don't even have the time to search for something else. You come right through the door and you bend me over and I listen to the sound of the buckle and then the hiss of the leather pulling through your loops." I was touching myself now. This was my porn. "You start on top of my clothes."

"What are you wearing?"

I actually had to look down at myself; I was in such a daze. What was I wearing? Faded 501s, black mules, vintage Rolling Stones-concert T-shirt, so old there were holes throughout the near-translucent fabric.

"Jeans," I told him.

"I start on your jeans?"

"Yeah, for the first few licks, and then you reach around my waist and unbutton the fly and slide down my pants."

"You've got on panties?"

"Yes," I told him. "Tuesday panties." I remembered

that. I'd changed after my second bath of the day. God, he would hardly have to touch me I'd already come so many times. I was more than primed. I was practically putty.

"And I use the belt on you through your panties?"

Clearly, his office door was shut if he felt so confident talking to me like this. Boldly. We rarely had phone sex. Jack was focused when on the job. But I supposed that his decision to establish a seven-day punishment had created the same effect in him the plan had in me. Longing. Overwhelming desire. When those Dom/sub pieces fit together, the result is a beautiful thing.

"Yes, Jack," I said, "but then you pull them down."

"I don't make you do it?"

"No, Sir. You pull them down." Christ, the thought alone of his hands on the waistband of my panties had me touching myself again, fingers thrust down my jeans, wishing he were here. Now. Surprised when he said, "I've got to run, Kid." And disconnected the line.

I'd moved to the living room, staring out the window, totally lost in my head, when the front door opened. I can be so slow. I needed a moment to realize he must have called the number from his car phone, downstairs, that he'd been playing me, as usual.

I tried to smile, tried to laugh even, loving the game, but Jack was moving. Jack was making my fantasy come true. Striding across the room quickly. Forcing me over the back of the big leather chair. Letting me hear that buckle. The melody of the sound.

Chapter Fifteen
Enough Pleasure

"I start on your jeans?"

"Yeah, for the first few licks, and then you reach around my waist and unbutton the fly and slide down my pants."

"You've got on panties?"

"Yes," I told him. "Tuesday panties."

Jack had listened to me create my own fantasy. He had paid careful attention. Even though my man was Dom to his very core, Jack was willing to let me direct from below this time. He whipped me steadily through my jeans, heating me with the well-worn leather of his treasured belt before reaching around and popping the fly of my 501s. I'd had these jeans since high school—and they were beaten in, perfectly broken. I felt him rake the worn denim past my slim thighs, felt him observing me for several seconds before bringing the belt down hard on my panty-clad ass.

All day long, I'd been craving this. All day long, I'd

wanted nothing more than for Jack to spank me, to use his belt on me, to fulfill the yearning that would not let me be. I hadn't worked. I hadn't done one single useful thing since I'd climbed out of bed. In my head, that was reason enough for Jack to punish me.

But Jack didn't need a reason.

There was something extra arousing to me about him using this utilitarian tool to tan my hide. Nothing dirty about a belt. He'd been wearing the expensive accessory unnoticed for most of the day. He'd talked to people at his office. He'd walked down the corridors. Think about this. He would have raised a few eyebrows had he been carrying a crop or a paddle. A belt was different. Anyone could wear a belt out in public. And now the Italian leather had a purpose far beyond keeping his pants where they belonged. Now that black belt was in motion, whispering through the air before connecting—solid and satisfying each time.

Jack's phone call had made my panties wet. He discovered this in minutes. When he decided it was finally time, when he lowered those Tuesday panties himself, he dragged one finger along the inner seam, feeling for himself.

"You're a little pain slut," he admonished me. "You know it?"

"Yes, Jack."

"Look how wet you get when I spank you. *Before* I spank you. All I have to do is tell you what I'm going to do, and you practically cream yourself. Isn't that so?"

He had moved closer to me, his heat my own, using the same tone of voice he had on the phone. His body pressed against mine, letting me feel how hard he was, letting me know how well suited we were for each other. Savagely suited. I was wet because he was punishing me. He was hard for that very same reason. I wondered whether he'd been as useless at work as I'd been today. I wondered whether he'd had to hide his erection behind his desk, or if he'd done what I'd done, taking a moment in the bathroom to care for his craving. I liked that image, enjoyed imagining him jerking off while thinking of me. Stroking his cock while fantasizing about whipping me with his belt. But I'm not a fool. I didn't ask. I kept silent and still, until Jack spoke again.

"You took over my head today," he said, and I felt both a swell of pride and a wave of uncertainty at his words. "You made it difficult for me to do my work. This is what you do to me."

He pressed forward even harder so I could feel his cock butting against me, demanding attention. The sensation made me sigh. Was I supposed to be sorry that he was as consumed as I was? I couldn't imagine that he wanted me to apologize. I guess he didn't, because all he said next was: "Prepare yourself." Then he backed up once more, and I looked down at the leather chair, and I grit my teeth. Waiting. As if I'd been waiting for Jack for years, not hours. But hadn't I?

Early on, Byron and I had attended a concert at the Hollywood Bowl. We went often—to hear jazz and rock 'n' roll legends. On this night, when we returned to his convertible, we discovered someone had tossed in one of those free newspapers you used to spy around town. This was in the pre-Internet era when a few keystrokes wouldn't get you what you desired. The paper was filled with pages of filthy ads, X-rated offers of massages by Swedish twins, complete with photos to make most men's fantasies come true. At the back were rows and rows of personal ads for the kinkier set, a whole column of offers for spanking enthusiasts alone. Byron went camping later that week, and the whole time he was away, I'd daydreamed about answering an ad. Calling up. Setting the appointment. Begging the person—I didn't care if it was a man or a woman—to take care of me. Byron had already denied this request, and I thought I might never have my truest fantasy fulfilled again.

I could get myself off simply by reading the ads. I took the step further in my mind—and my notebooks—sketching out a whole plot featuring a girl who couldn't get what she needed, who had to answer an ad to find true bliss.

And now look at me.

Just look at me.

Jack doubled the leather. He used exactly the right force. Over and over, striping me, spoiling me with the sensation. He drove all of the worries out of my head, all the old thoughts and nagging questions, all the fear. Until the only thing that was left was the sound of the belt, and my harsh breathing, and Jack telling me that this was only day number two in a week's worth of pain.

"You understand that, don't you?" A pause between blows.

"Yes, Sir."

"Every night, I'm going to come home from work and warm your bottom for you."

"Yes, Jack." I could almost come from his words alone.

"But that doesn't necessarily mean you'll win only one spanking a day. I hope you understood that."

Oh, Jesus...

"It means you get *at least* one..."

He was in motion once more, the belt coming down

harder, faster, and I had to focus not to flinch, not to cover my ass with my hands. What would he do if I failed him? What would he do to me if I interrupted his concentration?

"...I had to leave work early because of you..."

"Yes, Jack."

The belt was cutting hard now, and I felt tears welling.

"I took care of what you wanted this afternoon. But tonight—"

The crack of the belt sounded like a gunshot. This was the hardest blow yet.

"...tonight is going to be *mine*."

The tears were still there, sparkling in my eyes, but Jack had stopped before the crystalline drops could fall free.

I took a risk and looked over my shoulder at him, watching as he threaded the belt back through the loops of his slacks—oh, be still my heart—and realizing that he wasn't going to fuck me now. No matter how desperate I was for him. No matter what I said. What I did.

"Get those jeans off," Jack demanded, and even though I was confused by the request, I kicked out of the clothes, standing half-naked before him. He led me back to the bedroom, and while I watched, he got out a hateful chastity belt and fastened the cruel device into place.

"You've had enough pleasure for one day," he told me as he clicked shut the final lock. "I'm going to be in charge of the next time you come. Do you understand me?"

The very atmosphere between us had changed. "Yes, Sir."

"Now put on one of your skirts, and see if you can get some work done. I'll be back in a few hours."

He kissed me good-bye, then left the apartment. Left

me standing there, alone.

I shut my eyes. Knowing the afternoon was going to drag on. Knowing I'd have no relief until Jack finally decided to take pity on me. And knowing, based on the look in his eyes before he'd left, that mercy was a long way off.

Chapter Sixteen
Mercy Me

Mercy wasn't really in Jack's vocabulary. He could be kind, yes. He could be gentle, occasionally. But mercy, at least to me, implies taking pity on someone else. Showing leniency. And that concept rarely worked for Jack.

An example?

He didn't come home early, as I'd hoped. He stayed away past his normal arrival time. And as Alex was out of the picture—Where? Why? I had no idea—I was left to my own devices. I didn't feel comfortable going out. Not restrained in the chastity belt. I was fairly sure nobody could tell what I had under the skirt—but *I* knew.

I attempted to write, as Jack had suggested, but failed miserably. I couldn't lose myself in the characters, not when I was free-falling in my own world of sexual torment. Everything I wrote was about me, not about the people on my pages. They said things I would have said. They wanted only what I wanted. I like my characters to live in their own worlds. Ultimately, I gave up trying to force them to behave.

For a change of pace, I unpacked my bag for Paris and repacked, not making many substitutions, but taking up some time. When I had nothing left to do to distract myself, I poured a drink and sat outside on the balcony, watching the early evening sky slowly change colors.

When Jack did come home, I had no idea whether he would continue to work, as he had the previous night, or whether he would be ready to play with me. He didn't give me a clue by his expression or his words. So I was infinitely relieved when he walked outside with the key and set me free, allowing me to go to the bathroom and freshen up before meeting him in our bedroom.

I'd been anxious all afternoon. Daydreaming. Fantasizing. Now that he was back and waiting for me, all the fear came rushing through me once more. I stared at my reflection in the polished mirror over the sink, noting the flush along the line of my jaw despite the fact that the apartment was on the chilly side. Sensing the desire in my eyes. Tonight was his. He'd said so. But I wondered whether he knew how much that very concept turned me on—making tonight mine, as well.

He was ready for me by the time I got to the bedroom. Ready in a way I hadn't expected. What good was I? The supposed sex writer with an imagination that paled before my boyfriend's. Jack wasn't going to use his belt on me. Not tonight. He'd already taken care of me that way this afternoon. And this was his night—I kept reminding myself. What would that mean to Jack?

Apparently, it meant that we were going out. I saw that Jack had gone through my closet, had chosen one of my naughtiest PVC dresses, a sleek number with a bright silver zipper than ran the length from neck to hem.

He'd also put out a pair of high-heeled shoes, stockings, my collar, and a leash. He'd changed his own clothes, as well. I adored the way Jack looked in his suits for work, appreciated the way he dressed down in jeans and an old T-shirt or button-up Oxford. But when Jack wanted to go to a club, he had a style that managed to make me weak. Black. Always black. But not trashy. Not slutty. Not for my Dom. He chose black pants (sometimes leather, sometimes fine suit-like material), and either black long-sleeved shirts, or thin sweaters. Something fitted to show off his physique. But tonight, he was in black jeans and a black muscle shirt, and I thought he must be the sexiest fucking lawyer of all time.

While he watched, I stripped, then slid on thigh-high stockings, the dress, and the shoes. I didn't ask for knickers. If they weren't put out for me, then Jack didn't want me to wear them. I knew where he was taking me. Knew that Juliette would undoubtedly be involved. Wondered whether Alex might show up. It had been several days since I'd seen him, and somehow he had become the unspoken subject between the two of us. Fuck the elephant—Alex was the hard-on in the room.

"Ready?" Jack asked. This was a useless, stupid question in my opinion, a question that had no answer. No correct answer—or truthful answer, anyway. I had to say yes, or win Jack's wrath, but I was never, ever ready for something like that. Still...

"Yes, Sir," were the words that made their halting way past my lips. "Yes, Jack."

He gave me a final nod before attaching the collar around my throat himself, although he kept the leash in his hand, not making me wear the thing down the hallway, or in the elevator, which offered a tiny bit of relief. I couldn't imagine running into one of our hoity-toity neighbors while being dragged behind Jack like a petulant puppy. "Hello, Mrs. Evans. Woof. Woof."

We didn't head to the club right away. It was too early. Instead, Jack took me to dinner at a place on the beach, not seeming to give a fuck at how he'd dressed me. I could tell from the looks in some of the customers' eyes that they thought I was a whore. Jack didn't spare anyone else a glance, his attention focused solely on me. That's how he was. You do yours. I'll do mine.

With my hair this short, my collar was visible to all. I realized that my long tresses had offered me some semblance of protection that was gone now. Was that why Jack had wanted me shorn? To keep me from hiding behind my bangs, behind my dark curtain of hair?

"You're not eating."

"I can't—"

"I want you to eat, Kid."

I stared at him. Didn't he understand? My stomach was in knots. I couldn't possibly take a bite of the food he'd ordered for me.

"Especially with that drink." He indicated the whiskey I'd ordered, the same brand he favored. His tastes were blending into my own. I was learning from him. I'd be a connoisseur before long.

We agreed upon bread. Bread was the safest thing I could manage. And we lingered in front of the windows, watching the ocean until Jack decided it was time to go.

Juliette was waiting for us. I could tell. Even if she greeted the other guests with pleasure, with finesse, her eyes lit up when we walked through the door. Jack wrapped her in his arms in a way that sent fine points of jealousy shooting through me, but then Juliette offered me the same warm embrace, and I felt conflicted, my body responding to this woman in spite of myself.

"You're ready?" she asked me, and I turned to Jack, worry fresh in my eyes. Juliette laughed at my obvious fear. "You didn't tell her?" she said to Jack, chiding him in a way I'd never survive if I tried. Doms have their own secret language.

"I wanted it to be a surprise," Jack said, and he was grinning as well, so that I was the one left out. The one on the spot.

"Lovely," Juliette nodded. "That will make the evening extra special." With those words, she took me by the hand and led me away from Jack, led me into a room filled with bodies, toward an empty stage...

Chapter Seventeen
Don't Let Me Down

Jack had said a spanking a day for seven days.

That's what he had promised. That's what I was mentally prepared for. Today, he'd decided on two. I could handle two. But could I handle *this*?

Juliette led me through the black-clad crowd and up the steps of the bare stage. Not entirely bare, truthfully. There was a spanking horse off to one side and an armless chair dead in the center. I could feel eyes on us as she pulled me after her, and I refused to look out at the audience, refused to acknowledge the masses awaiting a sinful performance.

"Jack thinks you're ready," she said, turning to me, close enough so that I could hear her, even though her voice was soft.

"Ready," I echoed, feeling as if I were lost in a fog. Was I ready? Would I ever be truly ready for the things that Jack wanted? What if I said no? What if I turned and pulled away? She had the leash in her hand, but I could unclip the end from the collar, couldn't I? Would the crowd stop me? Would they block my escape? The thought both frightened and excited me, the image of those strangers out there, holding me in place until Jack could claim me. Oh, sexy beast—my imagination can surprise even me sometimes.

Juliette's eyes stared directly into my own, and I could tell she was attempting to read my thoughts. When she smiled to herself, I caught that she knew I wouldn't run. She was the one to unclip the leash. She was the one to tell me to take off my dress.

My heart pounded painfully in my chest. I felt as if I couldn't breathe. Where was Jack? Why was Juliette giving the orders? Yet even as the questions flooded quick and fast through my mind, I found myself obeying. My hand reached the silver tab at my neck, and in seconds I'd pulled the zipper from top to hem, so that the dress fell open, revealing the fact that I was both braless and panty-less. Once I let the dress slide all the way off, I was clad only in the stockings, heels, and collar.

You know those dreams you have of being back in school naked? The ones were you're standing on the quad in your birthday suit and there is no place for you to go? (Please tell me I'm not the only one who endures these nightmares.) Those visions pale in comparison to what being nude in front of an audience actually feels like.

That's when Jack took the stage. What had he been doing? Greeting his friends as if simply a guest at some kinky cocktail party? Observing from the wings? He nodded to Juliette, stroked her hair in a way that sent fresh green flames burning through me, and then he dismissed her with a tilt of his chin.

"I told you tonight would be mine," he said, his voice

as low as hers had been, but somehow loud enough for me to hear over the raucous noise of the crowd, the music playing, the sounds of moans coming as if from far away. At any other moment, I would have tried to hear the sex sounds. I would have started to write a mental story to accompany the noises. Not tonight. "You understand what I meant better now, don't you?"

"Yes, Jack."

"Here, you call me 'Sir.'"

Oh, sweet Jesus. *Sir. Yes, Sir. Whatever you want, Sir. I won't let you down, Sir. If you put your hand between my legs and touch me, you'll feel how wet I am, Sir. All for you, Sir. Everything for you, Sir.*

I stared down at the stage floor. This was probably the most difficult space I'd ever been in before. Naked in front of so many strangers. I claim to be something of an exhibitionist, but this was different. This was painful before the pain even began. "Yes, Sir."

"I gave you your fantasy this afternoon, didn't I? I made every frame come true."

He wasn't moving forward. He wasn't starting. He was forcing me to have a discussion with him while people I didn't know checked out the colorful tattoos on my naked skin, observed the lift of my breasts, the shaved region of my pussy. Were they judging me the way people do? Did I pass the test? I wished I were the sort of girl who could pull off a swoon, who could convincingly sink to the floor in a Victorian faint, one hand to the forehead, the other to the heart. But Jack would know. He'd catch me faking. So I stood, as erect as I possibly could, as proud as I could manage, and I focused solely on Jack's face.

"Yes, Sir."

"And now, you'll give me one of mine."

That was all he had to say to change the way I felt about the mood. I was giving *him* something. And I lived to give Jack whatever he desired. Rarely did he ask. Usually, he simply took. This was different. He was showing me a bit more of himself, he was revealing the man behind the curtain—and that man wanted to punish me on a stage, in front of not only an audience, but witnesses. People who would see us. People who would understand what it meant when he led me by the wrist to that frightening armless chair. He sat down and draped me over his lap, getting me in the position for my second spanking of the day.

"I don't care if you cry," he said, one hand rough on the back of my hair. "I don't care if you beg. This isn't about your needs."

"Yes, Sir," I spoke meekly to the floor.

"In fact," he continued, obviously relishing every single second he made me wait for the pain to begin, "I *know* you are going to cry. I know you are going to beg. And I can't wait to hear those pitiful sounds..." Spoken not only like a Dom, but like a sadist.

His hand connected for the first time then, jarring me, and I shut my eyes, knowing people were watching, sensing a shift in the room. This was different from anything we'd done before. We hadn't traveled down some long hallway to a private area, or at least a more secluded region. We were in the main room, on a main stage, and Jack was putting on a show with me as his more-than-willing prop.

There are times when I am immune. There are times when I'm so wet that the pain slides off me, that I can't feel it. Sometimes, when Jack fucked my ass, he could slap me as hard as he wanted, and I wouldn't even flinch. Afterward, I'd be surprised by the bruises he'd left behind.

Then there were times when even a light tap would drive me to tears. I can't quite explain the difference. Is it all about the headspace? Or are my nerve endings not wired the same way other people's are? On this night, every spank resounded throughout my entire body. Every time Jack's hand connected with my naked ass I had to regroup. It was as if he were reaching inside me, touching something within me that he hadn't found before.

I was infinitely aware of those people watching, and I knew that an over-the-knee spanking was probably the most mild form of foreplay for everyone concerned. Yet I knew we presented an interesting tableau. Jack was a Dom's Dom. He was unyielding, instinctive as an animal, sensing changes in me, knowing my limits without me ever having to explain. Knowing how to take me past them.

He had planned well this evening, because after what he must have considered a warm-up, I heard footsteps on the stage. I didn't turn my head. I didn't dare. But I heard Jack say, "Thank you, baby," and I heard Juliette's voice respond. The next thing I knew was that kind of fire that only comes with totally unexpected pain.

She'd brought Jack a paddle. One with studs. And the first blow made me squirm, so that Jack had to compensate, holding me firmly around the middle to get me back into position. He didn't say a word, he only continued, that wicked weapon landing again and again, until I was crying, as he'd said I would, until I was murmuring over and over, "Oh, please, Jack. Please." Not saying "stop," because he and I both knew that "stop" didn't mean "stop" at this point. (That's why so many people have comical safewords. Artichoke. Zebra. Antarctica.) But I was unable to keep quiet. Forgetting to call him Sir.

Forgetting how to behave like a good girl. I was sure the subs in the audience were looking at me with a critical eye, but I didn't care. The tears hit the floor, but Jack didn't let up. Only when my motions became true thrashing did he push me off his lap, stand quickly, and lead me to the nearby spanking horse.

"Oh, god," I gasped, not realizing, not meaning to, and Jack shot me a cold glare, but said nothing. He waited, silent, until I draped myself into position, and then he buckled me in place. I tensed immediately, checking the bindings to see if he'd left any give, any slack. He hadn't. My Jack knew what he was doing.

There was less talking out in the audience now. Less of the chatter, of the ambient noise. Because Jack was reaching his pinnacle. I could sense it, and clearly, the watchers could, as well.

I'd been with Nate at the club months before. I'd been public with Jack. But this was different. This was center stage. This was like a class in Exhibitionism 101. I was thankful for the bindings, grateful for the inability to fight. Yet Jack's need to bind me made me intensely fearful of what was to come. He wouldn't have buckled me in if he hadn't thought he needed to.

Fear always manages to turn me on.

Juliette was back, this time coming around the spanking horse to stare at me. Ah, fuck. Was she going to watch close up, deny me my ability to hide, to mentally disappear? It seemed like this was the case. She had given Jack something else, some other weapon of destruction, and now, she stroked my face, she gazed into my eyes, she let her thumb linger on my lower lip, so sexy, turning me inside out. And then Jack pulled me back to him, his voice no louder than a whisper. "Kiss her."

The people were watching. They were waiting. I had no way to run, no place to hide.

"Kiss her, Samantha. Don't let me down..."

Chapter Eighteen
Meeting in the Middle

Juliette was lovely. This Dominatrix was the type of well-chilled blonde who tends to make me nervous. She wasn't a dumb beach bunny. She was as icy as Jack's blue eyes. A martini in motion. And she wanted to kiss me. Or she wanted to please Jack. I didn't really care the reason. The way Jack had bound me allowed me to raise my head, and I closed my eyes and kissed her.

The room seemed to spin.

Not because of the lust rushing through me. Not only because of that. But because Jack waited for that precise moment to employ his next toy on me. He'd chosen a flogger, and he started slowly, echoing in a manner the way Juliette was kissing me.

Gently.

Lips to lips.

Lingering.

I fell into that sweet softness that only really comes with the very first kiss. Or the very first taste of a first kiss.

I wanted to hold her, wanted my wrists free so that I could drag her to me, so that I could cradle her face, stroke her glossy platinum hair, devour her. I understood she was Domme—a female equivalent to Jack—and I was sub. But something in her kiss made me want to take charge. Does that make any sense?

Maybe the fact that Jack was hurting me through this, maybe that's what gave me the faux feeling of power. He wasn't using full force. Not yet. The flogger stung my skin as Jack gained momentum, and yet the pain didn't quite manage to reach me. I was focused, intensely concentrating on Juliette. She laughed at me as she took a step back, out of my reach. Then she licked her bottom lip, and the look she shot me was more of interest than of mild amusement. I lowered my head, unable to contain the frustration that crested through me.

"You've got a wild one here, Jack," she said, taking another step back. "She'd break those chains if she could." As if I were King Kong and she were Fay Ray.

Jack didn't answer with words, using the flogger more seriously now, crisscrossing over my naked skin. The tool had many tails to lick and flick over my throbbing ass. The way I was bound, legs slightly apart, meant that sometimes one of those tails would catch me between my legs, and that would make me moan, to the obvious thrill of the groundlings. ("Whip her pussy!" I heard someone cry.) But I no longer cared about them. I wasn't shy anymore. I wasn't fearful or embarrassed. I wanted two things: to kiss Juliette and to come.

Seven days, he'd said. Seven days of spanking. And this was only day number two. How would I ever survive?

The pretty woman returned to me after a moment, and she was the one to cradle my face. She was the one to care for me the way I longed to care for her. Confusion floored me. I felt as if I no longer knew who I was, what I wanted. But when she undid the tie at the front of her beribboned top, unleashing her breasts and setting them free, I understood.

I parted my lips again. I suckled first from one nipple, then the other, all the while accepting the slow, steady rhythm of that fierce flogger against my skin. Juliette leaned her head back, delighted by my mouth on her. She sighed, and my own body responded. I was giving her pleasure and that brought me one level closer to climax, until Jack let loose of his toy and stood behind me. "I said *kiss her*," he reminded me, his voice breaking through my sexual haze. "What do you call this?"

I turned to look at him over my shoulder, and he gripped my chin in his hand, glaring at me. I'd assumed that Juliette knew what she was doing. That I had permission, somehow. That we had permission.

There was silence in the room. The very light seemed to still.

"You want her?" Jack asked next, and I tried to read the answer in his eyes, but saw nothing. All I could see was a mirror, a reflection of my own pathetic longing. "You want her," Jack said next, and it was no longer a question. "Fine, Kid. You have her. Here."

And he released me from the spanking bench, and I saw that while I had been faced away, some quiet minions had brought in a padded table. Silently. On wheels. And Juliette was already on the table, waiting, ready to put on a show for the crowd. Jack pushed me, teetering on my heels, and I walked to the table and climbed up with her, hesitating for one final moment as I looked back at Jack.

He nodded at me, his expression still unreadable, but

his approval now clearly given.

Juliette was wearing a full skirt of dark velvet, which she lifted to show her lack of undergarments. I was naked save for those few accessories. Together, we met in the middle, and I kissed her as I'd imagined. Kissed her as I'd longed to.

Yes, I'd been with a woman before. Similar looking, actually, but not so similar acting. Ava had been far more interested in pleasing Charlie than focusing on the two of us. On what we might do if we were left to our own devices. Juliette had no such qualms. She let me kiss her, and then pushed me down to the split of her body, leaning back so that I could have full access to the honey-slicked treat between her thighs.

For one moment, I hesitated. If Jack were in this position, doing precisely this to Juliette, I wouldn't have been able to handle the scene. I would have cried, or fled, or melted away into a puddle of pure liquid jealousy. But Jack was close by, and he had given me his approval, and I wanted to taste her. I'll say that as plainly as I can. I wanted to climb inside of her. I don't know what power she had over me. Perhaps because I'd seen Jack whip her once upon a time. Perhaps, we were connected in that way. I don't know.

I could smell her arousal, the tang of sex in the air. I knew what she would taste like when I brought my mouth between her legs, when I used the tip of my tongue to gather up the dew waiting for me. I hadn't felt this urge in me to be with a woman for quite some time. Now the desire was screaming in my head.

With the audience watching, with Jack right there, I put my hands on the silky skin of Juliette's thighs, spread her wide open, and bent to dine.

Chapter Nineteen
I Can't Stand the Rain

There was movement then. I felt a firm hand on the back of my neck, Jack's hand, pulling me by the collar. A black satiny curtain had come down on the stage, and Jack, by himself, had pushed the wheeled table out of the way. Apparently, a second "act" was taking our place. There were sounds of displeasure from the crowd, followed by a burst of noise—throbbing techno music had come on loudly. But I couldn't think about what was going on out there, could only pay attention to the fact that Jack had a choke hold on me, was pulling me off the table, pulling me to my feet.

I felt dizzy, as if he'd grabbed me up from being underwater too long, and Jack seemed to understand my physical state, lifting me into his arms, carrying me along some corridor...but to where? And where was Juliette?

Questions filled my head. Was he unhappy with my behavior? Was this one more test, like being told to kiss the waiter in New York, or tell that cruel Dom my safe-word at the club, or invite Alex into our world? Or had Jack scripted the entire evening, and this was simply the next step?

With his strong arms around me, all I could do was set my head on his shoulder and wait.

He took me a different way to the same room we'd been in once before. Alex had been seated in the bondage chair. I'd been positioned like a songbird in a gilded cage. And Juliette had been spread out on the table and cropped for her pleasure. Now, the room was empty, no goons needed to encage me. No Alex watching. Jack shut the door behind us with his foot, and then set me down in front of him.

And still I waited.

Jack paced the room, confusing me. I was the one who liked to pace. We'd momentarily traded roles. He seemed on the point of speaking, but he was taking his time, formulating his words. Was this what he looked like when he was in court? Or, more likely, when he was preparing to go to court, gathering his thoughts before presenting a case to the jury?

I'd never thought of him like that. Never tried to imagine what his world away from me must be like. The power he held, the other sorts of games he played. But now, I could see the vision of him. Could appreciate how others might view him. Jack truly was a force. He radiated a type of dominance that seemed to come from his very core. With me nearly naked in front of him, I felt as if Jack were about to make a case against me.

Christ, had I let him down once more? Was I meant to have refused to kiss comely Juliette? Had he wanted me to go on my knees and beg him not to make me join her...so that he could whip me more for my disobedience, giving the audience a longer show? I would have done that had he told me so. I hated to fail him.

Jack surprised me, lifting me up and setting me down on the table. He stood between my parted legs, and he kissed me, his hands roaming all over my body. Touching and stroking, finding the welts, the parts still sore, and pressing a bit harder here, so that I trembled in his embrace.

He kissed me, the way I said you only kiss that first time—with the intensity, the excitement of the blush of the new. But this was different. We weren't new, yet I felt as if in some way I didn't know Jack at all.

Without a word, he spread me down on the table, and he took the same place I'd hoped to take with Juliette. He got between my legs and he licked me there, and god, I cried out at the sensation, the sweet way he played me with his lips and fingertips and tongue. Knowing precisely how to continue. Understanding that after such a serious session of punishment, I could take just about anything. He sucked hard on my clit, making my muscles tense. He used two fingers on either side of that throbbing button, so that I was quickly out of my head, teetering on the precipice.

Why was he doing this?

I don't know. But I understood he was rewarding me, and I let myself float in the waters of iridescent pleasure. Let myself bask under the kind ministrations of Jack's knowing tongue. He licked me purposefully, tracing dirty pictures over my skin. He used his hands, spreading me open, combining the rough with the smooth, a prickle of pain from his short nails digging into the tender tops of my thighs. This wasn't our daily sport, but when Jack decided to go down on me, he gave me everything I've ever craved.

While I arched my back and spread my legs, Jack licked long and slow. My hands were useless at my sides until he paused to say, "Touch me."

I petted his hair. I grabbed his shoulders. I let him know with my hands how I was feeling inside—how he was making me feel. I still had no idea why he had ended the show with Juliette, but at this point, I didn't care. I took great breaths of air, and I shook the table as he worked me. Would people hear us if I got loud? I didn't know. I couldn't be sure. Did Jack want me to make noise? He didn't say. So I did my best to be strong and silent as he brought me to climax for the first time, those circles overlapping, the pressure true perfection—and then he pulled back and watched as those magical vibrations transformed me.

My head went back. My body tensed and relaxed, and I sighed deeply, once again feeling as if I'd emerged from the inky blue depths of a deep, wet pool.

Then Jack was up, and pacing once more, and I gazed at him, feeling completely different now. Feeling as if I'd been happily drugged with some form of opiate. Sleepy hazy. A sleek feline curled up in a warm yellow sunbeam. Until Jack said, "I understand now."

"What do you mean?" I asked him, not knowing if he'd mind my question, but taking a risk just the same.

"I thought I wanted you to fuck her, to lick her clit like a kitty, to make her come while everyone watched, but I couldn't handle that."

I stared at him, more confused than ever. She was a tool in my mind, like Alex often was. How had the scene changed for Jack?

He shrugged, as if I'd spoken the query out loud. "You looked so hungry for her, my sex vampire, so intense, and"—now he stepped forward again—"I guess I only want you to look that way for me."

Jealousy. It's a dangerous drug. It's a cruel aphrodisiac. Watching me part Juliette's thighs had awakened something fresh and dangerous in Jack. I understood now what made him pace, what disturbed him so, was that his emotions had betrayed him. He'd had a game plan, and even though everything was working as expected, he'd been the one to demand a change in course, a sharp turn of the wheel before we went over that cliff together.

I looked into his eyes as he waited for my response, and I found myself afraid of what I saw. In some way, he blamed me for this, for what he could only consider a sign of his own weakness. And this meant he would punish me for this unexpected burst of emotion. Of that, I had no doubt.

But maybe not right now. Right now, Jack was taking off his clothes. Right now, Jack was binding me to the padded table, wrists over my head, ankles wide apart. Right now, Jack was going to fuck me, was going to show me who was truly in charge. Yet, even as he climbed up with me, I saw the look on his face that let me know sometimes even Jack wasn't quite so sure.

Chapter Twenty
Why?

I posed the question before, tongue in cheek, yes, but still:

How do you make a sadist?

I don't spend my time pondering this query too often, don't worry so much about the flip side of the coin, either. What makes a masochist? What makes a sub? Oh, fuck. Who knows, right? You can agonize. Or you can go forward. But that little voice whispers every so often—why? A tiny tremor reverberating, growing louder as the days get colder, as the nights get longer.

Why?

Jack fucked me with every part of himself. I was bound. Tight and firm, without any ability to actively participate. But I felt what he was doing. Taking me as hard as he possibly could. As if to wipe away any of his own nagging questions. To erase them with the brutal force of his body on mine. I don't even have to say how much I enjoy fucking this way. Jack's cock was like steel inside me, hitting me hard and fast, making me whimper as the climax built. Jack's was the most perfect cock I'd ever had, so suited for my body it was like we were made for each other. Physically poured into molds that would fit so intricately well together. No factory error here.

But once again, this was different. Jack thrust inside of me, his muscles tense, over and over, and yet...and yet... he didn't come.

I knew his rhythms by now, could predict when he would speed up, or slow down, or stay still within me for a moment, to feel my body tighten on his, to win the velvety vise of my inner embrace. But not tonight. Tonight, everything was skewed, turned on the side, flipped upside down.

He climbed off me, let me loose, and then he stood and looked at me, and I knew he was planning, plotting, and I knew to stay silent, to wait. Still that question grew louder in my mind:

Why? Come on, Jack, why?

There was no Sir at the end of my query now. He was Jack again. But why was he like this, with the need to test me every step of the way, not always seeming to understand that sometimes he couldn't pass those very tests himself? I watched him, warily, understanding that Jack was on a mission now. He was proving something.

To me? Perhaps.

To himself? Definitely.

The room was filled with deliciously deviant devices, and a normal girl would have been fearful of what Jack might come up with. I don't pretend to be normal. In fact, I no longer am able to muster that ability. Crops, and whips, and belts, and paddles, pain, and danger—these are my aphrodisiacs, and I love them. I was excited as Jack slid back into his slacks and roamed the room. Would he put me in the chair he'd used with Alex? Would he bend me over that spanking horse once more? Would I find myself up in the cage, watching what—I could only guess?

Jack lingered at each part of the room, sensing my eyes on him, knowing that I could still feel the last few kisses of the flogger on my bare skin. How far would he go tonight? How much would he take from me?

Or were those the same questions Jack wanted to ask me? How far was I willing to go for him? How much pain could I withstand? That's the thing about boundaries. You think you have them, and then they move. You believe you know your own limits, until someone breaks them down. Tonight, I felt as if I were the one to push Jack's, and that's why he was now wandering through this chamber of torturous devices, trying to find his balance once more.

As before, the room was well heated. I wasn't cold or uncomfortable. Could stand there for hours. I admired Jack in his pants with no shirt, how fit he was, how attractive. He'd reached that horse once more, and this time, I walked over to him. This time, without a word from Jack, I bent myself in position. This was a different type of spanking bench than the one onstage, where I'd been partially upright. This one bent me in half in an upside-down *V*, and I clutched on to the lowest rung, holding myself without needing to be bound, parting my own legs.

Jack didn't ask me what I thought I was doing. I felt him watching for a moment, and I steadied myself. I knew, somehow. I don't know why.

"Your belt," I said, my voice husky, "just like earlier."

"Why?"

"Because," I told him, crazy talk this, daring as all get out. But somehow I knew what to do to make this evening right.

He put one hand on my bare skin, so hot already, so primed. Yet I was in that place, gone from the pain already, where more would only elevate the pleasure cycling endlessly through my body. Oh the heady Zen of pain. And he was in that place—this was the part I understood without knowing how I knew—where he needed more, needed to give more, in order to reach the end.

In my mind, I saw him lift his belt. In my head, I saw the way the leather looked driving through the air.

He didn't whip me long, only meanly, as if in a frenzy. The belt seemed to become a part of him. His breathing grew low and dark. And truly, we both knew why. Yes, we did. Juliette. Strange as that sounds. He whipped me because I wanted to please him by eating out his blonde friend, and because he couldn't face my very obedience to his own commands.

When he stopped, the rewards began.

On his knees behind me, Jack parted my asscheeks and licked between them. He traced circles around my rear hole, wetting me with his tongue. I knew how much Jack liked to rim me. I'd never dare talk to him about this particular kink, never query him about why he liked to lick my asshole. But I grasped the fact that he did, knew the act made him as hard as it made me wet. He spent a good long time lubing me with his tongue, spearing me with his fingers, opening me up and stretching me out. Each flick of his tongue on my asshole won me a lightning bolt of pleasure directly on my clit. I'm so wired for anal.

After Jack got me exactly how he wanted me, I thought for sure he'd take my ass. But no. He left the room for a moment, and I remembered the adjoining bathroom. I heard the water running and then Jack returned and I felt the lube. He made sure to oil me up until the liquid was dripping out of my asshole before splitting his slacks. He pressed the head of his cock to my back door and waited. I wanted to beg him to go forward, to fuck me. I wanted to demand that he give me what my body needed. But I knew my role better than that, knew I should not test him any more. Not tonight.

He waited longer than I would have thought possible, knowing how turned on we both were, and then he pushed forward. He let only the head of his cock rest inside me, and I felt my muscles squeezing him automatically. Welcoming him. Even if I didn't verbally beg him to take me, my body had a will of its own. He inched forward, so slowly, achingly slowly, and I nearly went out of my mind with my carnal needs.

Fuck me! I wanted to scream at him. *Fuck my ass! Fuck me hard!*

Until it was as if he woke from a slumber, and he began to move, taking my ass, speeding up until he was drilling me in the same manner he'd fucked my pussy, thrusting powerfully inside me. In a burst of silvery pleasure, I came, and Jack followed one beat later, filling me up, grinding against me.

Afterward, I felt wrung out, as if I could sleep for a week. Jack was different. Jack was electrified. He found me a robe in one of the drawers of the adjoining bathroom, and he put it on me himself. He led me back through the club, without pausing to speak to anyone, led me to the car, drove me home in near silence. Yet the mood was different. The mood was light.

"I lied," he said, when we pulled into the garage. I turned to look at him, startled by the comment.

"I said tonight was mine," he reminded me, and I nodded. "But, honestly, tonight was ours."

Chapter Twenty-One
Three Sunrises

And you're saying: "Well, what the hell is Jack going to do next?"

Right?

Or you're saying: "He said, 'A spanking a day, for seven days.' And then on day number two, he whipped the hell out of you at a club. What type of person could keep up an intensity like that under pressure?"

But I'm surprised you'd even have to ask.

On the third day, Jack was still in bed with me when I woke up. The coffee was made—a fresh cup waited for me on the bedside table—so he'd already been up, but had come back into the room.

"Meet me at the office," he said as I blinked myself awake. "After work. I'll give a call to tell you when I'm finished. When I'm ready."

I nodded, then rubbed my eyes.

"Your outfit is in the bottom drawer," he said next, and I looked over at his dresser, then back at him. "But don't open the drawer until I call."

Now, he had my full attention.

"I'll know," he said, standing up so that I could see he was already fully dressed, missing only his jacket. "Don't even think that I won't." He looked at me, the warning in his eyes, and then said, "Work today, Sam. Sit down at your desk and do your work. Or go out to the café and write. I'm going to ask you about that, as well. And I'll want to hear the truth. Don't let me down."

"Yes, Jack." Were these the two words I said most often in our relationship? I think so. Way more often than "No, Jack." That's for fuck sure. My eyes returned to his bottom dresser drawer. How would he know if I peeked? Jack seemed to guess exactly what I was thinking.

"I'll know," he said, and this time, he laughed. "Do you doubt me?"

I shook my head. Of course, I didn't. Not at this point of our relationship. But there is a whole current of curiosity that runs through me all the time. I believe every good writer possesses this quality to some extent. We want to know what makes people tick. We want to know what makes things work.

We want to know what's in that fucking bottom drawer.

Jack came closer and kissed me, lips warm on mine, and then he left for the day. I found myself lonely. Found myself actually missing Alex. How crazy was that? But I did what Jack said. I showered and dressed myself in a comfortable outfit. You want to know how I always seem to remember what I wore? Sometimes, I noted the clothes in my diaries. Sometimes, I took self-portraits with a Polaroid and stapled them to my notebook. I've had characters do the same thing. I don't consider this vanity, only a form of self-expression. And for some events, I simply have an ace memory. I know what color panties I wore to the prom: satin, coppery bikinis. I know what I was wearing on my third date with a movie star: stretch navy-blue pants with the word FREE high up on the left thigh, a mint-green short-sleeved button-up top with antique lace at the collar, and white Keds with no laces. We went to a ballgame in New York and watched the sun set over the stadium. I know what I was wearing, but I can't remember who was playing.

On this day, I wore jeans—jeans for me spell safety and Byron hated me in jeans, which might be why I own so many pairs of them. I wore a too-tight red SEX PISTOLS shirt with a black vintage cardigan. And I wore leather boots with attitude, so that each step was more of a stomp, and each stomp reminded me that what I really wanted to be doing was going on my knees in our bedroom and pulling open Jack's bottom drawer.

What could possibly be inside?

Why did he want me to meet him at his office?

What was going through Jack's mind?

Was he upset because of the events of the previous night? Or did he feel satisfied, soothed by the fact that I had obeyed his wishes? Wishes he wasn't entirely sure he'd wanted to come true.

I brought my notebook to the café, as Jack had suggested, and I worked on a new synopsis and a short story. During this time, as well as reviewing sex toys, I had a dozen pieces published in several magazines. I was lucky enough to fall in with a handful of female editors; my first and favorite had plucked me from the slush pile and given me a chance.

Maybe because Jack had told me to write, I was able to

put my brain in gear. I don't really know why the words came this day when they'd refused the day before. But I filled my pages and watched the world rumble by on Beverly Boulevard. And then I stopped by the salon to see Elizabeth, who always made time for me if she didn't have a client.

Elizabeth took my mind off the drawer by driving with me to a twenty-four-hour drugstore, where we could spend hours gossiping and trying on makeup. She told me the latest about her love life, and she probed me about mine, but I wouldn't share the details. We played the afternoon away, until finally I could go back to the apartment. Finally, I could walk down the hall, sit on the edge of the bed, and wait for Jack to call.

Chapter Twenty-Two
Color Me

How did I spend the rest of that evening?

Praying for the phone to ring. That, and thinking about how Jack could possibly find out if I peeked early, if I opened that drawer to see what might be in store for me.

How would he know?

What would he say?

Would things be better for me or worse if I disobeyed?

That was easy to answer. If I failed on this, undoubtedly, there would be no spanking, or some unexpected deprivation punishment along the lines that Jack liked to play with. And having him *not* touch me was so much worse than anything he could do to me with his hands, or belt, or paddle.

So I sat on the edge of the bed, phone at my side, and I stared at the dresser and waited. But then a new thought occurred to me: maybe Jack had chosen one of the outfits I already owned. Perhaps, if I looked into my closet and saw what was missing I'd be able to guess what lay hidden in the drawer. As I began to search through the clothes in my wardrobe, the phone rang.

If it's a sales call, I told myself, *I will hunt down the person and kill him.*

Jack said, "You been a good girl?" No "hello." No "What's going on?"

"Always," I said, and Jack laughed.

"What did you do today?"

I told him that I'd written and hung around with Elizabeth and spent more than a hundred dollars on low-end cosmetics, a feat even I was embarrassed by. How many tubes of merlot-colored lipstick do I actually need? There is no correct answer to that question.

"You ready?" he asked, interrupting my nervous chatter.

"Yes, Jack."

"Go ahead. Open the drawer."

I was trembling as I bent down and pulled open his bottom dresser drawer. Inside was a wrapped present. So he hadn't simply chosen clothes I already owned. I ripped into the packaging and pulled out a photo of Jack's secretary, and then dug deeper and found an outfit nearly identical to the one she was wearing in the picture. Jack knew my fantasy of working for him, but failing. And yet he had taken this fantasy a step beyond. I wasn't going to be any secretary. I was going to be...Tracey.

She was redheaded, taller than me but built along similarly slim lines. In the photo, she was wearing a black to-the-knee skirt, cream-colored blouse, and black blazer. Super professional. She had a similar hairstyle to mine, but hers was a natural coppery red, which explained the bob-style wig in the package. I wondered how Jack had explained his request for the photo, but I put the thought out of my mind. And then I wondered about Jack shopping for clothes. These weren't sex clothes. This was a real outfit. He'd had to go—I checked the label—into an Ann Taylor boutique, explain my size to a salesgirl, describe his desire. Somehow this struck me as kinkier than if he'd gone to an erotic store and purchased a replica of this outfit in vinyl.

"You understand?" Jack asked.

"Yes, Jack."

"The office should be empty in about two hours. I'll call you up when I want you to arrive."

I waited, knowing there'd be more instructions.

"You don't call me Jack," he said, voice soft.

"No, Sir."

"You don't greet me like you normally would. I expect professionalism all the way to the end."

"Yes, Sir."

He hung up the phone and I spread out the clothes, making sure I'd gotten everything from the drawer. The stockings and garters, patent leather penny loafers. And then, because I couldn't help myself, I looked under Jack's own clothes left in the drawer, his cashmere sweaters in different colors, spying an envelope at the very bottom, my fingers actually on the crisp paper before I pulled my hand back out and slammed the drawer shut.

This wasn't a silly game for me. I never was a big fan of make believe or dress-up. And now Jack expected me to act the part of his secretary, expected it because I'd shared this exact fantasy months before. But could I truly pull this off?

I slid into the clothes, which fit like a dream, then added the wig. Instant transformation. Somehow, the wig dissolved my inhibitions. Wigs are magical like that. I did my makeup to look like Tracey's in the photo, gazing at the picture, understanding this was taken at some sort of office function. She wasn't smiling in the picture, but she looked poised and professional.

When the look was complete, I stepped into the shoes and waited for Jack.

He called after the cleaning crew had finished his floor. It was late by now, and he had to let me into the building himself. I followed him down the long empty corridor to his office, aware of how empty the place felt without the constant human bustle. How loud even the most muffled noises sounded to my ears.

In Jack's office, he handed me a notepad and began to dictate. I'd worked in offices before—most notably (and poorly), at a huge architecture agency on Wilshire Boulevard, where I'd never actually managed to wrangle my mouth around the tongue-twister-like title of the three partners' names. I knew the drill of acting professional, even when feeling completely out of my league. I took the best notes I possibly could, and when Jack turned me loose to type up the letter, I actually headed toward Tracey's desk, thinking he meant for me to get to work, and feeling somewhat surprised when he blocked my path.

"You smell divine," he said, sounding so much like my Jack, not the lawyer Jack, that I forgot my role.

"It's Safari," I started, and his eyes hardened. Stammering, I tried to regain control. "Thanks, Mr.—" I tried again, but he said, "No, call me Jack."

Oh, dear lord. What was his plan? He'd specifically told me *not* to call him by his first name. So this was a test.

"Mr.—" I tried again, but he shook his head, backing

me toward the couch. This wasn't my fantasy at all; it was going to be his. I felt a metallic tightening in the pit of my stomach. Suddenly, I understood. He wanted me to fight him. I could tell that now. And, Jesus, from the look in his eyes, I didn't think it would be all that difficult to muster fear.

"You've been doing such a good job here, Tracey," he said, keeping me from moving. Easily holding me in place with the muscular bulk of his body. "I thought we should move our relationship up a level."

"Look, I'm flattered," I said breathlessly, putting the notebook between us. "But, you know, I live with my boyfriend. I don't think of you that way."

"You could though. Couldn't you, Tracey? You could think of me in lots of different ways. Boss. Lawyer. Master."

I shut my eyes. Jack was managing to make me believe he could be like this. That was terrifying somehow.

"My boyfriend knows I'm here," I said, trying harder, getting desperate as Jack's hands started to unbutton my blouse. "He's going to pick me up in a few minutes. He won't forgive you..."

"Drew's out of town. I heard you telling Danielle earlier. So don't lie to me, Tracey. I can always tell when someone's lying." He chuckled. The sound sent a cascade of fear over me. There was no humor in that laugh. "It's why I'm an excellent lawyer. Lie to me again, and I'm going to have to punish you for it."

Spanking Day Three.

That's what this was. And we were almost there. Almost. But not quite.

I bit the insides of my cheeks, thinking quickly. Jack's hands were in my shirt now, cupping my breasts through my bra, and part of me wished I could simply lie back on the black leather sofa and let him ravish me. But that's not what Jack wanted. He wanted the thrill of the chase. He wanted to force his way in. Yet his fingertips were having their way with me. My nipples were hard already, and I knew that when he reached into my panties, he would learn how wet he'd gotten me with this debauched fantasy.

"My roommate," I tried next. "She thinks I'm meeting her at a club tonight. She'll be worried..."

"Tracey, Tracey," he said, shaking his head at me, "You're such a good secretary, why can't you be a good girl? I heard you on the phone. I know your plans for tonight. A night of beauty by yourself with your favorite chick-flick movie. Though how anyone could watch *Thief of Hearts* more than once is truly beyond me."

Oh, my fucking god, his hands. I forced myself to slap them away, to squirm on the sofa to get space between us. Jack appeared to be supremely delighted with my reaction—the cat playing with the wounded mouse—and he snatched my wrists easily in one of his big hands and pulled me back where he wanted me.

"I said I'd punish you if you lied again." He acted as if this made him sad, as if pulling me over his lap was breaking his fucking heart. "And I don't go back on my word." Then he was sitting and I was in position, Jack hiking up my skirt, tearing my panties down firmly. In our normal life I would have accepted the punishment with as much dignity as I could muster; now I knew to fight. He landed several stinging blows while I thrashed as hard as I could against Jack, making him laugh out loud at the futility of my struggles. But when I felt him relax for a moment, I fought so fiercely that I was able to get off his lap and onto the floor.

My heart was racing. What could I do next? Where could I go? Before I had time to think, Jack was on me like a panther. "Bad girl," he said again. "Watch out. You might actually make me upset in a moment or two."

Then he was dragging me up and over the edge of his desk, pulling out his drawer and reaching for a wooden ruler. He had me pinned easily with one hand on my back as he heated my naked ass for me. There was no need for Jack to own a ruler in his world—a wooden, old-fashioned ruler that belonged in the desk of a headmaster at the turn of the century. No need except to spank me with it. I did my best to continue to stay in character. I tried to be Tracey. I tried to remember that there was a boyfriend at home waiting for me, that I was an employee and not a lover.

I struggled. I flailed so that items fell off Jack's desk to clatter on the floor.

But the spanking changed me.

Jack let the wood slap against my bare skin until I couldn't fight anymore. I was his, and he knew it, and the façade melted down around us. And then it was the two of us again. He pulled off my wig and stripped me out of those silly clothes, leaving me naked and striped, and undeniably his.

Chapter Twenty-Three
The Hand That Feeds

I'd never played games like that before, never even really thought about them. Being forced to do something wasn't in my personal fantasy files. (Although "forced" is such an odd term when I was being "forced" to do exactly what I wanted to do: bend over Jack's desk for a spanking. How happily, how willingly, I generally climbed into that very same position. Pet that I am.) But it seemed that Jack wasn't done playing this way, wasn't ready to switch gears to something new.

On the fourth day, he woke me by binding me down to the bed. Woke me up in order to fasten my wrists over my head, my legs apart. And then he fucked me, fucked me until I could sense the impending climax. Fucked me until I felt insane from the proximity of the pleasure—before roughly pulling out.

This was one of Jack's favorite cruel Dom tricks. He had an iron will. He could stave off his orgasm for so long I was left in awe. There are yoga practitioners I know personally who do this. They "recycle their chi" until they are blessed with an endless coil of bliss. Or so they say. Not me. I'm much weaker in the face of pleasure.

"We'll finish tonight," Jack said, heading toward the bathroom to take a shower. I could hear the water running, and I hoped he would release me before he left for work, but I had no idea. No way to know for sure. Not where Jack was concerned.

He was gone for a long time. Getting cleaned up. Setting the morning in motion. Back to the bedroom with a black towel around his flat waist, his face freshly shaven, hair still wet. He didn't look at me as he dressed, but I kept my eyes fastened on him, wondering whether he would give me any more hints as to what I was to endure. What I was to expect.

But no. Jack seemed perfectly content to have me bound, his captive audience, while he went about his routine morning business. He left the room to grab a cup of coffee, and came back, sitting on the edge of the bed while he sipped the fragrant liquid, not even offering me a swallow from his cup.

"We're going to play a little harder tonight," Jack said, regarding me with his face set, betraying no emotion. No clue as to what those words meant. He continued to drink his coffee while he spoke to me, and I wished even more desperately that I had a cup of my own, wished for something to help me chase away those last wisps of dreamland. Until his next words shook the remaining sleep from my brain.

"It won't be me tonight."

"What do you mean?" I asked, immediately scared.

"Last night, you were Tracey. Right?"

I nodded.

"Tonight, I won't be your lover. I won't be your boyfriend. I won't be Jack."

He unlocked the cuffs, undid the bindings at my ankles, and set me free. He was out the door before I could ask what those words possibly meant, leaving me to attempt to write. Leaving me to attempt to function. I was getting a bit better at this, to tell the truth. And by now, truly, I can write anywhere. On a plane. In a crowded bar. Surrounded by the chaos of daily life. I can tune anything out and write. Well-trained I am, courtesy of Jack.

On this day, I did my best, as I said, working hard on new stories for a collection, pouring out a good ten pages before I left the apartment and went in search of diversions.

He wouldn't be Jack.

Who would he be?

What did that mean?

I had no contact from my man all day long. When I returned home in the late afternoon, there was no message waiting. No news. I felt totally useless. I didn't know what Jack wanted me to wear or how he wanted me to act when he arrived. I only knew that he wasn't going to be himself—and those words echoed endlessly in my head.

If not Jack, then who?

I didn't work at an office. He couldn't arrive being my boss or my coworker, a male version of Tracey. He couldn't slide into a fantasy that mirrored the one we'd enacted the previous evening.

Dinnertime came and went without a call. I fixed a snack, but didn't eat. I played music, jumping from one band to the next, restless and ill at ease. Unable to really hear the sounds emanating from the speakers, because I was focused so deeply on listening for Jack's key in the lock.

The lights of Sunset grew brighter as the sky turned dark. And still no word.

Finally, I decided on a bath. That would relax me. He hadn't told me to be ready at a certain hour, after all. Had given me no instructions to obey—or to fail to obey. I poured in a capful of silky bubble bath. I settled myself with one of my battered (but beloved) books. I started to soak. It was after nine, but I was doing my best not to check the clock every few minutes.

When I heard the front door open, I opened my mouth to call out his name before I remembered: he wasn't Jack tonight.

Was that why the sounds were different? Not the normal noises of him entering the place and tossing his jacket to the chair. Not the familiar sounds of him pouring a glass of his expensive whiskey, opening the sliding door, stepping out on the balcony, as if to survey his domain? No, the front door opened stealthily, and then there was quiet. I held my breath for a moment, reached for the towel, started to get out of the tub, to dry myself.

The front door shut, a soft click, but there were no more sounds.

He'd warned me, hadn't he? He'd come home tonight. We'd finish the morning's adventure tonight. But he wouldn't be Jack.

And he wasn't.

When I got the towel around me, when I opened the door, he was standing there, in the hall, waiting. He had on black, all black, sweater, jeans, boots, leather gloves, mask. I saw his cool blue eyes through the holes in the second before he pulled the towel off me and flipped me around. That's when I got it.

Fight. He'd liked my spunk the previous evening. I hadn't given the action much thought, trying as I was to be Tracey, to think the way she might, to come up with excuses as a way to ward off her lecherous boss. But this was different. I was me tonight, and *he* was someone else, and I sprinted away from him, feet slipping on the polished wood floor, trying to reach the bedroom before he could.

But Jack, the athlete, was not even a beat behind me, holding the door open with his foot so that I couldn't shut and lock it, pursuing me to the corner of the room and grabbing me up in his arms. Easily carrying me back to the bed.

I struggled for real this time. Knowing that's what Jack wanted. Knowing he craved the animal pleasure of taking me. My fists beat his chest, but he had no trouble tossing me onto the mattress. Still, getting my arms over my head was a true fight. I worked hard to escape, nearly managing at one point to scramble off the other edge of the bed, before he got me where he wanted me, yanking both of my wrists up and cuffing one and then the other. I was lost now, I knew it and Jack knew it, but I still kicked out, still attempted to ward him off.

There was almost no sound between us during this whole time. Just the ragged noise of my breathing. The panting as I tried to get away. And then Jack, binding me face down and whispering to me. "Nice, very nice," as he stroked his gloved hand along my spine, down my naked ass.

Did he mean he'd liked the struggle? Or was he pleased with the way I looked, my body still damp, my muscles alive beneath the skin? My heart felt as if it would explode out of my chest as he used those leather-clad hands to part my asscheeks, tracing his fingertips down the valley there.

Oh, fuck, oh, fuck, oh, fuck.

But before he could, before he would finish what he'd started in the morning, we had business. This was Day Four, after all. First, there was…the spanking.

Chapter Twenty-Four
King of Pain

From the start, I thought Jack was taking pity on me. He spanked me with his gloves on, but not as hard as I expected. Not as long as I would have thought. The feel of the leather against my skin sent shivers through me. I've always had a hard-on for leather, and the barrier turned me on intensely. But Jack didn't spend too long with the punishment, didn't allow me to lose myself in the sensation.

Why?

At first, I didn't understand, and then I realized that he simply couldn't hold back. With one quick tug, he undid his slacks and got behind me on the bed. Surprising me like an intruder had turned him on intensely. He didn't have to explain this with words.

His cock told me all I needed to know.

But I was caught off guard by how easily he slid inside of me. My thoughts had been on hold since he'd first appeared in the hall. Or, rather, my thoughts had been entirely focused on two concepts: flee and then fight. I hadn't considered how aroused the scene had made me, my pussy so slippery wet that he drove in without any additional stroking or petting, any need for teasing, for sweetness.

Foreplay that night had been Jack dressed as an intruder.

Fucking was like a five-alarm fire.

He thrust so hard inside of me, and my body responded automatically, easily. And yet, even then—my nerves jangled, my thoughts unclear—I had a feeling that a simple fuck wasn't what Jack had in mind.

And I was right. He got his cock nice and wet, and then, with his gloves still on, he spread my cheeks and pressed the head against my asshole. I felt one of his gloved hands grabbing the back of my hair, his fingers searching for purchase, yanking my head back.

"Does your boyfriend fuck you like this?"

What did he want me to say? I took the safest route I could think of: I would not answer. I owed this stranger nothing. Not one fucking thing.

His cock was sliding in, slipping forward, and I bit down on a moan. But Jack didn't want me to be excited. He wanted me to be scared. He yanked harder on my short hair, and now the groan of pleasure turned to a fierce wince of pain.

"Come on, slut. I asked you a question. You don't want to make me angry."

"Yes—" I choked out. "He does."

"I thought so," Jack said, now thrusting hard, driving inside me without pause, all the way until skin met skin. He didn't release my hair. He was still in that mask, still all in black, and I was naked and shining from the bath, wet and ready. "Why else would you have all those kinky toys?" Jack continued. "The cuffs, the bindings permanently fastened to the bed. Perfect for a slut like you."

Again the moan of pleasure threatened to escape from my lips, and as if Jack were inside of my skin, feeling the same sensations I was experiencing, he knew to pull harder, so that my head was tilted back, so that I could look into his eyes.

Oh, Jesus, Jack's eyes. Generally, I could read his mood, or at least grab a clue, based on their changing hue, or the crinkles around them, or the way he'd raise an eyebrow. Softening a statement. Hinting at a joke. But now, all I could see was that arctic blue, and I had no way of knowing what he wanted from me. What he needed me to give.

I played quiet. I listened carefully, the whole time, Jack thrusting inside my ass. His hips rocking.

"Does your boyfriend tie you down every night? Does he worry that you might try to leave him?"

"No," I said, quickly, automatically. "I'd never leave him."

"So how's he going to feel when he finds out you've been with another man?"

I like to believe that I'm a smart person, but Jack was throwing me curveballs. And I couldn't keep up.

"That you've been fucked by another man..." he continued, making things worse.

I was stammering, at a complete loss, pleasure coming in waves now from the way he was fucking me, but fear the steady counterpart, keeping me teetering. I was paying close attention to Jack now, understanding that he had a plan. That he had a script.

"What do you think he'll say?"

I shook my head. Or, at least, I tried. Jack's fist in my hair kept me from fully being able to make the gesture. There were tears in my eyes now, because I felt lost. What did he want? I'd never fuck another man. Yet, he was not Jack tonight. He'd made that perfectly clear. So in our twisted surreal way, I *was* fucking another man.

"He loves me," I said, the only thing I could say. "He loves me."

"A slut like you? You think so? You think he really does?"

The tears were spilling freely now. I was stunned by how quickly he'd made me cry. With almost no pain at all.

"I know he does."

He let go of my hair then, gripping my hips firmly to keep me how he wanted me, driving into me with abandon, his cock so hard, his clothes rough on my naked skin. I felt as if he were tearing me in two, splitting me open, and I wished I could collapse, curl up, hide. But I was splayed, and Jack was taking me. Not only fucking me but taking me.

When he came, he came inside me, and then he pulled out and climbed off the bed. I had no thoughts of what he'd do next. Of how he might become Jack once more. No thoughts at all. I closed my eyes as I heard him leave the room, heard the front door open and then close

Where was he going? When would he be back?

It was moments later. The door opening once more and Jack making those familiar noises, the ones I'd listened for while in the tub. I heard him pour his drink. I heard the sound of his footsteps approaching the bedroom door, his voice, "Sam? You back there?" And I shut my eyes even tighter.

I knew it was Jack who'd fucked me.

I *knew* it.

But as he pushed the bedroom door open, I felt the first true wave of fear.

What was he playing at now?

He hurried to unbind me, and I saw that he was dressed as he'd been in the morning. He was in his work clothes, so different from the all-black outfit of the intruder. He didn't say a word as he rubbed my wrists, as he stroked the tender skin to soothe away the marks. He was Jack again now. No mask on.

His blue eyes shone. There was humor in them, and although I was afraid he was going to ask me what was going on, fearful that he would make me tell him about the man who'd broken into the apartment, he didn't say a word.

When he kissed me, I understood there was no need to be afraid, or even to pretend to be afraid, but somehow I knew that this form of play had now joined our X-rated repertoire. Jack liked the scene too much to let the first time be the last.

Chapter Twenty-Five
Crazy Little Thing

Paris loomed up in front of me, but I could not focus on the trip. Couldn't spend my hours lost in delicious daydreams about where we might go and what we would see. Couldn't page through the tour guides to search for places Jack might choose to fuck me. Instead, I focused on where we were currently. That's one thing Jack's game did for me. Kept me locked in the present, locked by the knowledge that I was now in Day Five.

There was no warning on this day. No drawer to open at a certain time. No clue as to what Jack's plans were. He'd promised me a spanking each day for a week. But because of the way he'd acted on the previous days, I had a feeling there would be more to tonight than a simple session over his knee.

And I was greedy. I wanted more.

During this time, I was writing my heart out—cheating my time between several different projects. That's how I always am. If you were to peek at my hard drive you'd see dozens of stories in motion, some mere opening lines, working titles, others half finished, or needing only a spit and polish.

I did my best to put in solid writing time, and then I wandered Sunset, visiting the stores that inspired me, entertained me. Book Soup. Tower. I lingered at the Sunset Strip Tattoo Parlor—not even thinking of adding to my collection, but fantasizing nonetheless. I had no idea how Jack would react to me getting a tattoo without consulting him. I'd inked myself before hooking up with Byron, but I knew my ex never had liked the art on my body. Nowadays, it seems everyone has designs adorning their skin. But when I was a freshman in college, uncovering tattoos on a lover—especially a shy girl like me—was still fairly unexpected.

I bought myself a new outfit at a store that no longer exists. A dress for a vixen, all shiny black vinyl with a neck-to-hem zipper. Something Jack would like, I thought. Left to my own devices, I didn't feel comfortable simply waiting for him. I had to present myself. I had to be prepared, even if what I chose was wrong. Even if how I dressed was the opposite of what he was looking for.

I had to try.

Back home, I did my makeup carefully. I have full lips and I like to wear dark lipsticks. True blue reds that make me look as if I've spent the past hour eating cherries or licking a raspberry lollipop. I put on mascara. I fixed my hair. And then I slid into that slippery dress, poured myself in like a drink, and waited.

He'd come home late the day before. There was no reason to think he'd be early today, and he wasn't. No reason to think he wouldn't make me wait, when waiting for a spanking was almost as much of a turn-on as actually bending over and receiving one. I used my standard pass-the-time techniques. I drank. I listened to music. I organized items already in order. The phone rang a bit after eight, and I had just lifted the receiver, just heard Jack's voice on the line, when our front door opened, and I froze.

"You there?" he asked, but I didn't respond, didn't make a sound. It wasn't Jack opening the door, and I inched closer to the knives on the counter in the kitchen as I heard footsteps approaching. "Baby?" Jack's voice soft, crooning, and then the gloved hand around my chest, yanking me backward, the hissed voice in my ear to drop the phone, the sensation of being literally dragged away from the kitchen, pulled down the hallway by someone I couldn't see.

Was I scared?

He'd prepared me, Jack had. The previous night had been an introduction. But this was different. This wasn't Jack. For *real*, this wasn't Jack. The man hefted me over his shoulder and carried me to the bedroom, and I knew—body type, strong physique, even by his scent—that this was Alex. But I fought just the same. Kicking harder this time, trying my best to get loose. He'd caught me off guard in the kitchen, but I was prepared now. When he threw me onto the bed, I rolled off so that the mattress was between the two of us.

Alex had the same outfit on, or an identical one, to Jack's. Mask. Gloves. All black. Had I thought Jack's eyes were cold the previous night? They were nothing to the frozen glare that Alex was giving me now. He'd been gone, and I hadn't asked where. But now that I saw him, I could sense the anger toward me—the distrust or disdain, I wasn't sure. How had Jack wooed him back? With the promise of my submission? With the reward of binding me down and fucking me?

I wondered whether he could hear the beating of my heart. Wondered whether he could sense the desire flooding through me. I was surprised when he spoke. "You gonna fight me?"

I didn't answer.

"You think that's wise?"

Not a word.

"Wouldn't it be easier if you took that dress off yourself? If you acted for once in your life like a smart girl. Don't you think that would make life easier?"

"For you," I managed to say, still trying to figure out my options. (What options, right?) I had to get past him to reach the door. There was no way out except through that doorway. And from the way Alex was staring at me, I didn't think he'd give an inch.

He actually laughed when I spoke. He liked the response. "Yeah, it would be. I could tell Jack that you behaved—"

"He doesn't want me to behave," I said, moving so slowly forward, getting into position. I didn't think he'd noticed that I'd stepped out of my high heels, that I was leaning ever so slightly forward...

"What do you mean?" Alex asked, his voice calm. He was enjoying this. I could tell. He was playing with his food.

"He wants me to fight."

"You think?" Regarding me this whole time the way a hunter would. As if knowing that the prey would be a tasty treat, but deciding to let it entertain him for a moment first.

I was poised now. I was ready. "If you told him I gave

in, he wouldn't believe you."

"But it's going to work out the same for you," Alex said matter-of-factly, still standing there, watching me. "You're going to wind up bound to the bed. Your ass is going to be tanned for you the way you need it—the way you always need it—and then you're going to be fucked. Why not get onto the bed yourself? Why make me chase you?"

I heard those last words as I streaked past him, sliding in my stockings on the polished wood floor, heading for the front door. If I made my goal, where would I go? I had no idea. But I had to try. I flung myself down the hall, hearing Alex behind me, and then feeling Alex behind me, his iron grip around my waist, lifting me once more. He didn't carry me back to the bedroom. Didn't even wait to take care of me, flipping me over one bent knee, hiking up my dress, and spanking me. And still I fought, trying to push him off balance. Trying to win.

His voice had changed. "I gave you a chance," he said, steel-like and cold. "That's all I was offering. One chance. Now, you're mine..."

I shook my head, still struggling.

"I'm not yours." I had to get the words out. Even though Alex was wearing a mask, even though he was dressed like an intruder, he was still Alex. I couldn't give myself over to him. I wouldn't.

"Until Jack comes home, you are."

"No," I said again, struggling and panting to get away. Alex finally seemed as if he'd had enough of me. His very body language changed the way his voice had. He lifted me effortlessly and carried me back to the bedroom. He subdued me easily while he bound me in place.

"That's how he wanted you," Alex said, and at least his

breathing was a bit ragged, too. That fact gave me a tiny bit of pleasure. "You could have spared me a bit of effort, but instead you fought. And now you'll pay..." Yet even as he spoke, I saw the look in his eyes. I'd done the right thing. I hadn't given in. He couldn't sell me out to Jack. He would have to tell the truth. And I saw something else: he understood what Jack and I shared. He didn't have to like it.

But he understood.

Chapter Twenty-Six
Don't Worry, Baby

Alex had me exactly where he wanted me, but that didn't mean his job was finished. He opened Jack's toy chest and began feeling around. I wasn't scared. *Yet.* He'd bound me face up. I didn't think anything painful waited on the immediate horizon, but when he pulled out the red-rubber ball gag, I tensed. Alex seemed to sense my trepidation, because he came forward slowly—the trainer approaching the tiger—and I thought how only moments before, he'd been in the position of top cat. Now, even with me bound, he seemed uneasy about stepping too close to the cage.

I shook the few wisps of hair away from my face, stared at him, daring him. But I had nothing to back up the look. With my wrists and ankles bound, there was no way for me to fight other than spit at him, and my mouth was dry.

Alex buckled the mean contraption into place, and then he backed away from the bed once more and stared at me. After a moment, he pulled off the mask, and ran a hand through his short blond hair. He wasn't breathing hard any more, but I could tell the adrenaline was still coursing through him. Had to be. I was still practically vibrating from the fight.

Jack arrived too soon to have been calling from work. He and Alex must have intricately planned when the "intrusion" would take place, because within minutes, there were two men in the bedroom, both looking down at me, each with his own smug expression in place. I saw the way Jack looked at Alex, as if pleased with how he'd found me. "She give you a hard time?" he asked, as if already knowing the answer.

I stared fiercely at Alex, wondering whether he'd lie, and he shot me a sneer before answering. "Yes, Jack."

Jack appeared to be even more pleased. "And she was wearing that when you came in?"

"Yes," Alex said, and Jack turned his attention to me.

"Something new, baby?"

I couldn't answer verbally, but I nodded. I wasn't presenting myself as precisely as I'd imagined at the clothing store. The dress was rippled to my hips now, like shiny black water, and my garters, stockings, and black lace panties were fully exposed.

"You put up a fight?" Jack asked, focusing his attention fully on me, now. He was stroking me through the dress, and he didn't seem to expect a response. "I like that, doll," he said, softly, as if trying to mesmerize me. To make me relax. How could I relax? There were two men in the room, gazing at me as if I were dessert.

And besides all that, this was Day Five.

All I could think about was how Jack might spank me, and what Alex might have to do with that scenario.

Truth? I was intensely wet. It would only take a few quick strokes to get me off. But I didn't want an audience.

I only wanted Jack. Yet I'm enough of a die-hard Stones fan to know you can't always get what you want.

Jack slid the zipper down the dress, peeling the tight fabric away from me. He couldn't take the outfit off. Not with me bound. But he spread the vinyl wide, then ran his fingertips along my body, from the hollow of my neck to the basin of my stomach. I shuddered, his fingers raising goose bumps all over my skin, as if I were chilled rather than turned on, and Jack laughed. He loved how easy I was. I knew he could tell from the yearning in my eyes exactly what I craved, but he made me wait.

"Why'd you bind her like this?" he asked Alex, sounding casual, curious.

"She was struggling so hard. I got her in the quickest way possible."

This made me feel all kinds of pleased. I'd screwed up Alex's plan, if only slightly. Why was I feeling such animosity toward Alex? Because he'd caught me. And easily. Next time, I assured myself, the fight would be much more intense.

"I want her face down," Jack said, and Alex hurried to his side, lifting the chain of the cuffs from the hook while Jack undid the bindings on my ankles. They obviously thought I would continue to fight, but I didn't. I went limp as Jack positioned me the way he wanted me. Why bother struggling? There would be no use. How could I fight two well-built men, especially when I didn't even want to?

Jack stroked my hair, still treating me gently, and then he stood and spoke to Alex in a hushed tone and Alex left the room. I relaxed. It would be Jack and me, and I could handle whatever that meant. At least, I thought I could. Jack sat by my side, his warm hands running down my back, his voice a melody. "Don't worry so much, Kid.

Don't worry, baby." He laughed again when the door reopened, when I turned quickly at the sound, seeing Alex return with the kitchen scissors in hand. Jack cut the dress off me, not saying a word, until I was naked save for my underthings. He cut the panties off, next, and then removed the ball gag. I licked my lips, stretched my mouth in the seconds it was empty, before Jack slid my wet panties between my parted lips.

"Bite down," he said, "taste yourself. Taste that sweet honey."

With Jack, all alone, I would have been embarrassed, but aroused. With Alex, watching, I was mortified. I don't know why. He'd seen so much worse. This was the man who'd examined me. So what was my problem? Perhaps it was because he'd been AWOL. I wasn't accustomed to him being back like this. I had gotten used to the situation of being a duo rather than a trio.

Jack headed to his chest of devices and emerged with a toy, which he held behind his back. I didn't try to guess what it might be. I didn't want to see. Until Jack spoke: "You do the honors," Jack said to Alex. "You break her in."

And then, I couldn't help myself; I had to know. I turned my head quickly, in time to watch Alex hefting one of Jack's paddles. His eyes met mine, and he gave me a wicked smile. He was enjoying every second of the evening. To him, this must have been payback.

"I don't want her like that, though. I want her over my lap."

Jack was undoing the bindings once more, keys flashing. But now, I had to think. They'd wanted me to fight. Did I try it? Did I take a chance?

You tell me. Did I?

Chapter Twenty-Seven
Crash

Ah, you know me so well. I'm a good girl. Really, I am. With the best intentions, but the darkest desires. I want to be able to test my boundaries, but I want to discover that I can't get free. Since forever, I have held out my wrists to my boyfriends, showing them, "Here. Touch me here. Kiss me here." My fine bones offered up. Hoping that they will grasp the rest, figure out what that gesture means:

Don't hold my hand; hold my wrist.

Don't lead me by the hand; lead me by the wrist, drag me down the hall, my steps fast to catch up to your long strides.

I can turn myself on by touching my own wrists—the lightest of fluttering caresses—but when a man does that, when a lover understands, I nearly swoon.

This evening, when the bindings were on, I thought of freedom. Of testing. Of trying to fight. And no, I'm not a moron. I fathomed there was no chance of winning this situation. Not with two able-bodied, fully dressed men in the room. Where would I go even if I did make it to the edge of freedom? I was in stockings and garters. Outside wasn't really a possibility.

But still...

As soon as Jack had unbound me, I crawled away from him, because he was the one to watch. Alex wouldn't chase me without Jack's approval. I backed off the bed and shot down the hall. Once more. Déjà vu. Feet slippery in the stockings. No idea where I was headed.

I realized as I slid toward the living room that they weren't chasing me. They weren't pouncing after me, predators in pursuit.

I like to test my boundaries. But I like to discover that I can't get free. What did it mean that Jack wasn't hot on my tail, that he hadn't told Alex to hurry up and grab me, to drag me to the bedroom? My question was answered as soon as I reached the front door. Hanging from the handle was a cane. A new one. Silvery in the light. Metal? I sucked in my breath looking at it, feeling as if I'd run into an electric force field. Some invisible barrier that would not let me through.

Then I heard Jack's footsteps behind me, and I backed away from the sound and from the front door, finding myself slowly moving toward the balcony. Jack didn't rush toward me. Didn't act surprised that I'd fled the room. He wasn't smiling, but he didn't appear upset or angry, or any of the emotions I expected. In his hands were a pair of jeans and a T-shirt. My clothes.

Slowly, he walked toward me, and slowly I backed away, until I was pressed against the glass doors leading out to the balcony.

"You don't have anywhere else to go," he said, almost as if he felt sorry for me. He was right. I could slide open the door and stand nearly nude out on the balcony. Or I could press myself against the glass so hard that I might shatter the door or myself. Or I could wait to see what Jack would do next.

"I thought you might run," he said.

I swallowed hard.

"That's why I left the present for you to find." His eyes flicked over to the cane, and a trickle of fear worked through me. I had no idea what that thing would feel like, but insecurity decimated me. Especially at the way Jack was acting.

"Do you want to run away?"

My breath caught in my throat. "No, Jack."

"Are you sure?"

He put the clothes out on the sofa arm. I stared at the pile and then back at him.

What was he offering? What was he suggesting?

"Run," he said, "if you feel you need to. Run."

My heart was pounding so loudly that I couldn't even think straight. I felt as if I had a rhythm section sounding off in my head. Cymbals. Xylophone. Cowbell.

Jack took a step closer, and I pressed back even harder. "Run," he said, softer now, more menacing. "But I'll find you. You understand that, don't you? I'll find you. And I'll catch you. And you'll end up right back here, in the corner. Right where you started."

As he spoke, I flashed back to that first night in Jack's place, when he'd locked me naked outside on the balcony. When he'd unleashed the words I'd been dying to hear, desperate for someone to say to me. "Don't worry so much, Samantha. I need it, too." That night opened all the other nights we'd shared together. That night was pure in my head.

Was I running away from that? From Paradise? From salvation?

I looked at the ground, at my feet. I would not meet his eyes.

"Are you going to run?" He was close enough to me now that he could whisper and I could hear every word.

"No, Jack."

"So you're going to go back to the bedroom and climb over Alex's lap like my best girl, and let him heat your ass for you the way you deserve. Is that right?"

"Yes, Jack."

"And then you're going to lie down on the bed, and hold yourself still, and get ready for a taste of my brand-new toy."

My teeth chattered. "Yes, Jack."

"If you'd behaved," he said, so close now his breath was warm on my cheek, "then the cane would have been a present for another day." He was stroking my hair now, his hands soothing me. Running his fingertips down my neck, along my shoulders. I felt confused. All I wanted now was for him to fuck me. And yet that wasn't going to happen. At least, not yet. Maybe not for a long time.

Jack seemed to understand my desires. He cupped my pussy with his hand, and his fingertips sought out the wetness awaiting him, his middle finger stroking my clit so that I would have lost my balance if he hadn't supported me with his other arm. The pleasure was even more powerful knowing what pain I'd have to go through before I experienced relief.

"You're ready for me," he said, voice sweet. "I like that. You make me want to break my own rules. You make me want to lick you while you stand there, flip you around, lick you back here," he reached behind me to strum my asshole. His touch made me weak. "But first, we've got a bit of business to take care of."

He led me down the hall, his large hand tight on my wrist, making sure that I wasn't going to try to get free again. He led me to Alex, who was waiting, already seated on the bed, paddle at his side.

"I want her totally nude," Alex said, and I saw that there had been no doubt at all in his eyes that I would be returning to him, that I would be undoing the garter belt, sliding off the stockings while both men watched.

Then I was over Alex's lap, and he stroked my ass with his hand several times before using just his palm on my skin. Teasing me with the foreshadowing of pain before making that vow come true.

Chapter Twenty-Eight
Want

Alex spanked me while Jack watched, and I felt as if I'd slipped back through time. Back to the beginning. Enough days had passed since Alex had last placed a hand on me that I was nervous from the first strike. Nervous because I'd seen what awaited in my very near future. Nervous because I wondered what else Alex and Jack had discussed about their "intrusion" fantasy.

I also wondered why I'd assumed that Jack wasn't in touch with Alex. Why had I so easily been able to push Alex from my mind, to ignore his very existence?

Now, I couldn't ignore him at all. He used his hand repeatedly, and then, when I began to seriously feel the heat, he lifted the paddle and gave me a hard, fast ten. Too fast to count. Too quick to comprehend. I wanted to behave—not for him so much, but for Jack—and I did my best not to squirm or kick my feet. Alex didn't have to hold me in place, and his left hand was at his side. I don't know why, but I found myself holding on to his hand tight with my own left hand, gaining some sense of strength from that strange bond between us.

What was the bond?

We both loved Jack.

But the connection went further than that. We'd both been hurt by Jack, whipped by Jack. We both had a taste for pain—no matter if Alex was more comfortable switching from bottom to top and back again than I would ever have been. We both were transformed by the first blow, or perhaps by the promise of the first blow.

I felt electricity running between the two of us, and suddenly I knew what I required to get through the rest of the evening.

When Alex was done, Jack waited. He'd given me instructions, and he wanted to see if I would follow without a struggle. Obediently, I took up my position on the bed, but I locked eyes with Alex, and he seemed to read the expression on my face. Coming forward. So close. Offering both of his hands to me. I gripped them and lowered my head, hoping that Jack would allow this. Hoping that he'd give in to my needs. Would this equal weakness to Jack? Or strength? My body was tense, my muscles alive and waiting.

Jack didn't speak. I held my breath, feeling the heat starting within me, having no concept of what that new toy would burn like, but desperately trying to find the strength somewhere deep in myself to wait unbound, to wait unfettered.

There were no words. Jack didn't tell me to prepare myself. He didn't admonish me to behave. He simply started, and I felt as if my world had been turned upside down.

When Jack let the first strike land, I gasped. The sensation was so unlike anything I'd felt before. Truly different from your average cane. I shook all over and then tried in vain to find that place inside myself that allowed me to disappear. To dissolve. But Jack was on me again, lining a second blow right before the first, and there was no time. I shut my eyes so tight that ultraviolet stars exploded behind my lids. I squeezed Alex's hands as hard as I possibly could, undoubtedly causing him some mild discomfort. Still, the pain floored me. Had I experienced worse? Probably. No—definitely. But sometimes the quality of the pain doesn't matter. The ability to hide, or to seek, or to find that shining glow within yourself—that's what matters. And you either succeed or you fail.

I failed.

Jack hadn't told me how many strokes he would land. He might have planned on five. He might have planned on fifty. Didn't matter. I pulled away.

"Samantha." This was issued in a warning tone. I opened my eyes to see Alex looking at me curiously. He was surprised by my behavior—or misbehavior.

"I can't—"

Why? I don't know. As Jack had called me plenty of times, I'm a pain slut. I should have those words tattooed on my body—or branded on my ass. PAIN SLUT. I lose myself. I slip down into the sticky mess of it. But this was different.

He struck again, before I could turn, and I realized why he'd let Alex hold my hands. Alex wasn't merely giving me something to grasp on to, he was keeping me in place, even after Jack had told me I wouldn't be bound. Hell, I'd bound myself. I felt trapped, desperate, the pain ripping through me.

"I can't," I said again. But those two words contained

no meaning. I *could* do anything Jack asked of me, and he'd asked me to take this. But for some reason, the fight that had gotten into me, the reason I'd fled down the hall, that spirit hadn't left me. And I found the will to struggle.

Alex's grip transformed, from holding my hands, to holding my wrists, and crazy as this sounds, when he did that, my whole world changed once more, righted itself. From lost in pain, to lost in desire. Touch my wrists. Oh, yes, baby, touch them. I say this, again, in that hushed, confessional tone that draws people in close to me: my wrists are the most sensitive part of my body. This explains why I own so many pairs of cuffs—leather, metal, traditional, heavy, high-end, utilitarian. I looked up at Alex, and saw the expression on his face. He was enjoying himself, the smug bastard. I looked at his body, and saw his hard-on, easily outlined against his slacks, and wanted something more.

Wanted Jack behind me.

Wanted Alex in front of me.

Wanted payment for the pain.

Or for the pleasure.

Just plain wanted.

Jack let go of the cane at five. He climbed onto the bed, hoisting me onto my knees, preparing to take me from behind. He didn't give me a word of instruction, but I knew instinctively what to do. I fumbled with my hands, pulling open Alex's fly, releasing his cock. As Jack slid inside of me from behind, I drew Alex's rod into my mouth and began to suck, still feeling shattered. There's no better word for the jagged sensations crashing within me. But with the two men bookending me I also felt somehow more like a winner than a loser.

You stone-cold Doms out there are saying that I

should have asked for permission before using my mouth on another man. How dare I? Who did I think I was? I respect that. I ought to have looked over my shoulder and asked Jack if I could blow Alex, if I could part my slicked-up lips and let him inside the warm wet heaven of my mouth. But Alex simply being there seemed sign enough that Jack wanted the boy to claim his space once more in our bedroom, that he wanted Alex back in our bed. And Alex's hard-on was sign enough that he wanted my mouth to pleasure him. And the three of us became entwined in that silver-lit room. In the center of the bed. With me, the link between them. Bracketed by my two handsome men.

Alex thrust forward, and I drank him down. Jack drove his cock into me, and I enveloped him, welcomed him. I was being used by my two men, and I could not get enough. The sounds I made, the whimpers around Alex's cock, the moans when I paused in the blow job long enough to take a breath—those sounds were musical. The melody of arousal, the harmony of total bliss.

I used one hand to cradle Alex around the root, holding him firmly while I tricked my tongue up and down his sensitive skin. Then I sucked him down once more, so that he was the one to moan. He was the one to sigh.

Jack was able to watch Alex's expression, and he could see how hard I was working to please his boy. More than that, he could feel for himself how wet this situation had made me. My body let him know—and more specifically, my pussy let him know—that I was beyond turned on. I clenched around him. I tightened on him. I squeezed and released again and again.

Alex came first, and I made the instant decision to drain him, swallowing every drop of his essence as he flung his hips toward me. Jack strummed my clit, so that I climaxed next, setting my face against the rumpled sheets and feeling as if I might dissolve into golden nothingness. Jack was last. He pulled out and came all over my hot, hurting ass, and then he rubbed his palm along my curves, as if delighting in the sensuous slide of his semen on my skin.

What's a happier ending than that?

Or if not an ending, then a beginning.

Chapter Twenty-Nine
Day Six

I was the first one up in the morning. You don't believe that, I'm sure, as I seem to be able to sleep like the dead, dream through anything. But I was up and out into the kitchen, to brew the coffee. To shower. To dress. Up and ready when first Jack, and then Alex emerged from the bedroom, a strange situation. An odd sensation. Who the hell did we think we were?

I've read articles on how to conduct a ménage. Supposedly, it's always best to use the third party like a tool. To have no emotions invested. But this wasn't any one-time deal. We were not so much a ménage as a triangle. And the main point of interest wasn't me, the way your average threeway would be conceived by your average romance writer—but Jack.

Jack was the focal point. Jack was the shining star. Jack was...staring at me in an unusual way. "*You* made the French roast?"

"I've made coffee before," I told him. I brewed several

pots a day when I worked for Jody, who appreciated his java hot, fresh, and black. Wasn't like I didn't know how to handle a Mr. Coffee.

"And you're showered?"

I pursed my lips at him. So I was up early. He didn't need to fuck with me. Except he was Jack. So he did.

"Everything okay?"

What was he asking? I looked at him, feeling confused as to the proper response. Sometimes Jack's questions ran deep. Sometimes they were simply questions.

"Fine," I told him, and as I said the word, I flashed back to the night before, to the way we'd ended up. No longer with me the connecting rod between my two men. No more pretending. Three lovers in bed. With hands everywhere. And mouths. With limbs overlapping. And pleasure like I had never felt before.

Yes, I had been in ménages previously. Yes, I had shared a bed with these two men as well. But there had been an honesty in the prior night's actions. An opening of a forbidden door. A diving into the turquoise deep end. A...

"You want to talk about anything?"

I shook my head. I didn't. I felt free. For no reason at all. Jack stared at me for another moment, and then he sipped his coffee and ran a hand over his short black hair, and stretched. He wasn't tense. I could tell that from every motion. He seemed pleased that I was awake, pleased to share the early morning sunlight with me.

"Show me," he said.

"Show you..." I echoed, not comprehending.

"Take down your jeans, and show me."

I turned around, lowered the faded denim, lowered the black satin panties, and Jack's fingers played immediately over the stripes still there in bold relief. The stripes left by his brand-new cane. There was pain in every touch of his fingertips on my naked skin, and there was bliss in each stroke as well. Jack played me so easily. So damn well.

"Day Six," he said before he headed toward the shower. "Don't forget."

And now I was nervous. Now, my feelings changed. I hadn't forgotten, but I'd thought Jack might let me off. After the toy he'd used the night before, I had hoped he might give me a pass.

I can hear your laughter at that.

I told you, I'm a liar. I'd known he would never go back on his word. How could he? He'd never break my faith in him. I pulled up my jeans as Alex wandered into the room, searching for the coffee, looking sleepier than either Jack or myself. We had a big bed. Everyone had enough room. But Alex didn't appear rested. He snagged a cup and headed out to the balcony, clad only in his black pants, no shirt. I followed him out and we stood and looked down on Sunset in silence. In only a few months, we'd created an uncomfortable history together, constantly testing each other, trying to gain the upper hand. Who had the power now? I had no idea. Alex sat down on one of the chairs and looked at me.

"We're spending the day together," he said finally.

"Yeah?"

His eyes gleamed. "Yeah. Day Six. Jack has everything planned."

He must have had everything planned from the start. Why wouldn't I have believed that Jack choreographed each day long before Day One had ever arrived for me? Why did I never seem to catch on, to catch up?

I looked at Alex again. Day Six. He'd said the words,

too. So he knew, as well. He knew that Jack had spent the past five days making sure that my ass was well punished before I fell asleep. He knew all about it. And with that statement, he climbed back on top. Alex wasn't the one lowering his jeans to show off a well-tanned derriere. Alex wasn't the one clamping his thighs tight together in anticipation of whatever might be planned for the day. No, Alex already knew. He knew what I did not. He knew the progression of the day's events, and he knew the outcome.

But I suppose I knew at least that much, too. The outcome? Me, over the lap of a dominant man, being spanked. Didn't know which hand would hold the paddle, or if a paddle would be employed. Didn't know if the spanking would be long and hard, or merely a wake-up call before sex. Didn't know whether I would cry or I would come. Or both.

I took a deep breath and looked back down at the boulevard.

But I did know this. It was Day Six. And I couldn't wait for the answers to all of my questions.

Chapter Thirty
Breathe

Jack went to work, and Alex stayed home, and I wrote. I've penned more than one thousand stories by now but am pathetic about keeping track of when each one was written. I have a portfolio, and I can take a guess. I was writing exclusively for a New York publisher at the time, as far as novels go, but I submitted the shorts to several publications. (Online wasn't really a big market yet. Yes, I'm that old, believe it or not.) I don't know what Alex did while I wrote. Puttered around. Read the paper. Made himself invisible. He reemerged only after I'd finished, seeming to sense I'd completed that task. (Jack never compromised my writing. He was insistent that what we did together would not interfere. In truth, what we did together only helped. How could I not be a better writer when I was living out my fantasies in real life?)

"He's meeting you for lunch," Alex told me. "And he wants you to dress pretty."

Pretty.

I try not to use that word too often in my work. What does "pretty" mean? Something different to every person. When I was a masseuse at a skin-care salon in Beverly Hills, we were required to wear pink and floral. That's what "pretty" meant to my boss. As you can imagine, I pushed the limits. Pink floral—skintight pants from Betsey Johnson and an itty-bitty halter. But what did it mean to Jack? I looked at Alex, hoping for clues, but he shrugged and went back to the living room.

My closet was filled with costumes. Even my everyday clothes had a theatrical air since I shopped mostly at vintage and thrift stores. Would a '60s cocktail dress be considered pretty? Would a white lace-trimmed vest count? I stood for what felt like an hour in front of my wardrobe, trying to decide, finally landing on a white pleated skirt, white blouse, white jacket. It was pretty, without a doubt.

Because I'm a rebel at heart, I wore the outfit with my patent-leather Docs, then I fixed my hair and makeup, and went out to find Alex.

He gave me a once-over and nodded, before leading me out of the building. He was my chauffeur today, a role he hadn't played in some time. But he didn't appear to mind. We hardly talked on the way to the restaurant. I had the feeling that he knew a secret, and he didn't want to give away a single clue. We drove all the way out to the beach, to a high-end restaurant, and Alex dropped me at the valet stand and pulled the car away, without any further instruction.

Feeling nervous for no real reason, I headed into the building.

Jack was waiting for me at the bar, and when he saw me, he smiled. So I knew I'd done something right.

"Lovely," he said, as he came to my side. "And a skirt like that. Couldn't be more perfect."

I'm smart enough, or I was well trained enough, not to ask "for what?" Perfect for what? I waited, knowing all would be explained in time. Trusting Jack that much. Trusting Jack always.

He didn't take me to a table; instead, he squired me to a corner of the bar and ordered us each a drink. "I don't have too long," he told me. "Maybe an hour. I didn't want to waste it on food. Not on Day Six."

I pressed my thighs together.

"We've done a lot together," he continued, sipping his drink. Jack never appeared affected at all by the alcohol. Not even by a midday drink. For me, the liquor went to my head, as Jack must have expected. "But we're falling behind in one of the ways I most like to play."

I continued to stare, feeling one of Jack's hands on my leg now. Feeling his fingertips slipping underneath the hem of the short skirt.

"Can you guess?" he asked.

Fuck. He wanted me to talk. I'm always so much better at listening. And what could he be going on about, anyway? As far as I could tell, we covered quite a lot of fantasy ground during our sexual exchanges. There were toys and costumes. Clubs and ménages. What *didn't* we do?

"I like to give you spankings when you earn them," Jack said, and I wished like hell he would lower his voice. He was talking in a normal tone, and although the bar wasn't full, there were people around. Jack didn't seem to give a damn. Did he ever? "And I like to spank you when I'm in the mood, or when you're craving one. But I think that I've failed you in this way..."

Failed. What was he referring to? I had no idea.

"You're not being punished enough in public."

I was going to leave a wet spot on the stool. I was going to soak my panties and my skirt and leave a puddle behind.

"We started off fine," Jack continued. "The garage at Jody's office. And we've had our fun in alleys, and the occasional parking lot. But my feeling is that you've grown a bit complacent. You don't think I will spank you when we're out..."

As he spoke, I wondered whether he was right. Was I complacent? Did I ever feel like I could get away with anything with Jack? No. Not really. But Jack had a prestigious job, and I tended to believe he wouldn't do anything that would come back to haunt him. He didn't care if I was flushed with mortification, but he wouldn't bring the embarrassment on himself. Why would he?

"...which is what I have planned for Day Six," he finished, and I realized to my chagrin that I had dazed out for the last part of his statement. What did he have planned? What had he said? I felt like a student who hadn't been paying attention in class. And there was nobody next to me to crib off. I looked at him, wild-eyed, as he put down money for our drinks and reached for my hand. Where was he taking me?

"That skirt is perfect," he said again, as we walked out of the restaurant together. "I couldn't have chosen a better one myself."

We were close to the beach...and the beach is never empty in L.A., but it wasn't too warm, so the crowds weren't thick. Jack strolled with me, hand in hand, until we reached a place where we could look down at the sand

and the ocean, the bike path, the gorgeous houses. The railing was made of wood, and Jack bent me over here, clearly not caring if anyone could see.

"Lift your skirt," he said. I looked at him, begging. I knew this spot well. I'd lived four blocks away from here with Byron. And of all the times I ran by on my morning jogs, I never once envisioned that I would be receiving a spanking right here. If someone had told my past self about the future life I'd be living, I wouldn't have believed a word. "Now," Jack demanded, and I flipped my skirt up in the back, closing my eyes as I did so.

"Don't hide," Jack instructed. "Don't pretend you're all alone. You're out in public, and I'm going to spank you. You didn't do anything wrong. I'm going to spank you because I want to. Because I've been thinking about this for weeks now, taking you out here, where people might see. Because I want you to get used to that thought. That it might happen anywhere. That I might punish your little ass any place I choose."

Why was he talking and talking? Why hadn't he completed his speech over our drinks? Standing there was torture, even if the girls down on the beach were far more scantily dressed than I was. They weren't being exposed in the same way. They weren't about to be spanked.

"Now your panties," Jack said.

Oh, fuck. I turned to look at him, considering pleading for mercy, and saw that his eyes were that chilliest of blue. Maybe this was a lesson in public exhibition, one that he considered lighthearted. But he expected obedience every step of the way. Our relationship hadn't changed. My hands were trembling as I slid my panties down to my knees, and then Jack started, smacking my ass hard with his open palm. If I'd been paying more attention,

I would have understood that he was shielding me with his body from the busy street, that the thick trunks of the palm trees nearby were concealing us further, and that someone would have to jog or bike directly past us in order to realize what was going on. But I felt as undone as I had onstage in his friend Juliette's club.

"Breathc," Jack said, breaking through my thoughts, and I realized that I'd been holding my breath this whole time. "Breathe," he insisted, and I sucked in a great gasp of salt-tinged air as Jack focused on a specific spot, his cupped fingertips slapping against the wetness of my pussy with each blow.

"You could come like this," he told me, not sounding the least bit surprised. "Remember that fact when you're trying to tell yourself you don't need this..."

How could he see inside me so easily? How had he known that I was fighting exactly that thought in my head? That I didn't need what he was doing? Putting me out there, where anyone I knew might drive past and see. That was a lie. I *did* need it. Just like Jack said. I needed every single second.

He didn't let me come, to my great dismay. He spanked me until I could tell that my ass was hot and pink, and then he flipped my skirt back down himself.

"Give me your panties."

I stepped out of them and handed them over automatically. Any slight breeze at all would have revealed both my lack of knickers and my freshly colored ass, but I didn't hesitate. Jack slid the underpants into his pocket, and walked me back to the restaurant, where Alex was waiting in the car.

"I didn't have time for lunch," Jack said as we got to the front of the building. "So Alex will eat with you."

I had to go in there, in my short skirt and no panties, my ass hot and throbbing, and dine with Alex, who must have known exactly what had taken place. I looked help-lessly at Jack, who only laughed.

He kissed me hard on the lips, and then said, “See you tonight. Alex will help you get ready.”

And he was gone.

Chapter Thirty-One
Secret Journey

"He took you up on the bluffs, right?"

"Yeah."

Alex's eyes were bright and interested. He wanted me to talk, to tell him what had happened, but I couldn't. I felt drunk, even though I'd only had that one glass with Jack. I felt off balance and unsure of myself, my place in the world.

It's not as if I'd never been out without panties before. Oh, lord, no. Jack had often taken me out in public with nothing on under my dress. He appreciated having a secret between the two of us. Especially, when we went out to the theater, or fancy events. But dining with Alex after being spanked by Jack—*having* to dine with Alex, I'll say, because I wasn't even the slightest bit hungry—that was almost the worst punishment of all. Alex knew what had happened—I could tell he did—and he sported that smug, almost smarmy look on his handsome face. The "better-you-than-me-look" I'd seen several times before.

But I could hardly focus.

Jack had given me more information than usual. He had planned the event, yes, but he had also confessed that he wanted to play more like this in the future. And *play* is such a fucked-up word for what we did together. Explore? No. He was teasing me. That's what this was. Teasing me with this seven-day game. Yet at the same time he was letting me know that there would be more public punishments in my future, and that they wouldn't all be choreographed like this one.

That's the thought that had me squirming on the chair throughout lunch. A long lunch, I should add. Alex was enjoying both his meal and my discomfort.

"Just a quick spanking?"

The people at the neighboring table looked sharply in our direction. I could feel their eyes on me, and I quickly turned to stare out the window. What was it with these men who liked to mortify me in public? And what was it with me? Why couldn't I get into the scene? Why couldn't I lean in and talk to Alex as if he were my best girlfriend in the world, sharing all the emotions that had flooded through me during the last hour. I could almost hear the conversation:

"He made me lift my skirt and take down my panties. He only used his hand, not his belt, but I was worried someone would come by and catch us. I could imagine what Jack would say if that happened: 'No problem, Miss. I'm just punishing my naughty girlfriend. Care to watch?' Or worse: 'Care to help?'"

But Alex and I weren't close like that. Christ, I wasn't close like that with anyone. I couldn't tell Elizabeth the truth about what Jack and I really did together. I couldn't tell my friends from school, the few people I knew from college. Or...well...anyone. There were no Internet chat-rooms to lose myself in. No confessional place for me to feel at home or at ease. Alex ordered for me, without even asking what I was in the mood for. I didn't say a word. I understood that his ordering had to have been a decision made my Jack:

Take her in there, grab her a lunch, bring her back home.

Sometimes I forgot that Alex was in so many ways a sub like me. He did what he was told. But that didn't mean he was immune to fucking with me.

"He use his belt?"

I choked on my water, but shook my head. It was as if Alex had read my mind.

"Really? I guess he's saving that for later."

This was Alex topping me, Alex showing off, flexing those baby Dom muscles. Was he trying to let me know that if I were nicer to him, more pleasant to him, he'd share information with me? I wasn't going to fall for that. I knew who Alex was—inside of himself. I knew. There was no way he'd tell me anything Jack didn't want him to. And there was no way that I was going to share with him what had happened by the beach. At least, not in the play-by-play format Alex seemed to be thirsting for.

That is, until Alex said, "You know he loves you."

I squinted at him, looked down at my plate, and then back at him. "Yeah." I did know this.

"Really loves you."

But what's love? What does that word mean? Why do we all crave those four letters strung together in that saccharine manner? I've written stories about the concept—oh, hell. Aren't *most* stories—erotic and otherwise—down deep at the soul about love? But I have had men tell me they've loved me, only to disappear, poof in a puff of smoke. And I've mouthed the word myself and not considered the weight, the meaning. Fuck, I wore a man's ring—a ring that the commercials tell us equals true love always—without shouldering the weight, carrying the burden.

"He's never been like this before—the way he is with you." Alex looked as if he didn't really want to be having this conversation with me, or as if he were saying the words with some difficulty. This conversation reminded me of our time in Griffith Park when Alex had asked me if I could love him. If someday, maybe, I could love him, too. "Take this however you will. He's different with you. And that's a good thing. As good as he is for you, you're good for him. You make him"—he hesitated before settling on the word—"whole."

I sighed. His words were well received, satisfying.

"You'll see," Alex said next. "Things...you know, things like this take time. Just trust him."

How those words must have cost Alex. I could tell that he'd prefer it if I were just another filly in Jack's stable. But now that I wasn't, I appreciated him talking to me. I was grateful, even if I didn't necessarily act that way.

When Alex finally asked for the check, he saw that I hadn't eaten a bite, had merely pushed my food around on my plate, like a little kid.

"You want to take that home?"

I shook my head. The waiter removed the plate and then brought the check. Alex paid in cash, crisp bills slid into that leather folder. He waited for me to stand, winking at me when I smoothed the skirt over my naked ass. He knew that I was praying I remained covered until we got to the car, praying a strong breeze wouldn't reveal my lack of knickers.

"We've got a few stops on the way," he said, and I looked at him for clues, but received none. As usual, Alex was loyal to his Master.

He drove us back on side streets, pulling up in front of my favorite—forever my favorite—lingerie store in L.A. I worship everything about this place. The pastel pink membership card you keep in your wallet. The fact that you have to be buzzed in. The panties and thongs and camisoles and corsets tacked to the walls. The cherry prints, leopard prints, marabou-trims; truly, the endless variety.

But shopping with Alex was different. On my previous excursions to this exotic emporium, I'd always drifted around in a daze until something caught my eye. Or many somethings. Throughout the years, I've actually shopped here with quite a few of my contemporaries—writers whose names you might recognize from spines on the same shelf as mine. But shopping with Alex was bizarre, because he was clearly a man with a mission.

He strode directly to a wall of panties and in seconds a helper was at his side. He began speaking to this gorgeously dressed salesgirl, pointing to the panties, and then to me. She went off in search of my size and returned with an armful of ruffle-backed panties in the patterns Alex had chosen. I wondered why Jack hadn't bought the items himself. Why had he sent me here with Alex? And why was Alex choosing items—so many different styles—without consulting me?

I decided to busy myself in the second room, drawn as always to the schoolgirl skirts and to the naughtiest cuts in the sweetest designs. I had a jumper and a two-piece, both plaid, in hand when a salesgirl started to help me, adding thigh-highs, going in search of the appropriate shoes. I'd actually managed to forget about Alex, disappearing behind the velvet curtains into one of the dressing rooms, when he called out for me.

"I'm not ready."

"You are," he said, following the sound of my voice.

"But I'm still trying things on."

"Today's trip wasn't about your needs," he explained, matter-of-factly, peeking through the curtain at me. "We have another place to go."

He had two bags with him, already paid for, and he was obviously impatient.

"But I like this one."

"You're forgetting something," Alex said, stepping even closer, half in the dressing room now. "You're forgetting that I have no problem punishing you in public, either. That I would have zero hesitation about taking you out to the alley behind the store and spanking that naked ass of yours. I know you don't have any panties to get in the way. I know he already heated your ass for you. But that doesn't mean I can't do close to as good a job. Don't forget who trained me."

I was hurrying back into my original outfit as he spoke, aware that he had done nothing to lower his voice, to spare me embarrassment.

"Can I at least put on one of the new panties you bought?" I asked.

"What do you think?"

I finished dressing and exited with Alex, pink-cheeked as we passed the salesgirls who gave me curious looks. I could tell that they thought Alex was in charge of me. What would they have thought if I'd explained that my boyfriend was Alex's boss? Or that we'd spent the previous evening in a bed together, the three of us joined in the most aerobically erotic ways?

Maybe they wouldn't have been shocked in the least.

Perhaps customers like us came through the doors every day.

But I don't know...somehow I don't think so.

Chapter Thirty-Two
Beauty

"This way," the photographer said. "Give me that look again."

I knew in school that boys my age couldn't see me. I don't mean that in any paranormal sense of the world, like I was ghost or a spirit. I mean that I was invisible to them. They couldn't see me in the halls. They never spotted me at dances. Of course, the boys didn't do much for me, either.

"You know what I want. That up from under thing you did with your lashes."

But one thing I have always understood—a fact that was hammered into me a long time ago—is that I'm not pretty. Not traditionally pretty, anyway. My lips are too big. My hair is too crazy curly. I hardly have breasts to speak of. Over the years, I've gotten past the desire to fit in with the blonde, buxom crowd. With the tall, leggy thoroughbreds. I'm fine with the way my hair falls into my eyes, with the way my full lips look slicked up with scarlet, with the fact that I can get away with going braless if I choose and hardly jiggle at all.

"Beautiful."

Still, posing for the photographer Jack had hired brought all of those miserable insecurities rushing back over me. But I'm getting ahead of myself.

That evening, we ended up at the Malibu house. The lights were already on and cars I'd never seen were parked in front. Alex, true to form, didn't explain a damn thing. We'd spent the afternoon together, visiting several unexpected locations once we'd finished lingerie shopping. I was relaxed—post-manicure and pedicure by my friend Elizabeth, and sporting a cool slick hairstyle. I felt at ease until Alex opened the door, revealing…

"Now, over your shoulder, chin down."

…a photo shoot. Photographer. Assistants. Lighting. Backdrop. Missing only one thing…

"And take off the bra."

…me.

"I don't get it," I said to Alex, watching the artists scurry around. "I don't understand."

The photographer strode forward, hand out, and said, "Jack wants some photos. And I owe him a favor. We decided to shoot here, because of the space."

This didn't make sense to me. Alex handed over the bags he'd bought. And yet the confusion lingered.

"Put on the first outfit, Sam, and get yourself together."

"*I'm* the model?"

"Of course."

"I'm *not* a model."

"You are today."

"But I'm not…"

"They're waiting."

And that was all the warning I got. I headed to the bathroom with the bags, feeling sick with nerves. What the fuck was this about? Why couldn't Jack have explained at the beach? Because he didn't like to explain. And if he'd told me ahead of time, I might have fled. Or begged him to spare me. But why wasn't he here, then? Why wouldn't he be here to give me confidence? To keep me company?

Alex knocked on the door.

"I'm not ready!"

"The cherry print," he said through the door. "I think that one is going to look awesome on you."

So he was a stylist now. I gazed at my reflection. This was why he'd had the makeup artist at Elizabeth's salon paint my face. This was why I now looked like a girl out of the '50s. My lips so glossy and candy-apple red. My eyes huge, lashes incredibly long. I reached into the first pink bag, ruining the neat tissue wrapping and pulling out the cherry-printed outfit Alex was referring to: ruffle-bottom panties, a matching bra, red fishnet thigh-highs with bows at the top done in the same cherry fabric, and stack-heeled red stripper shoes.

I dressed but didn't leave the safety of the large powder room. They wouldn't drag me out, would they?

Alex knocked again.

"Come on, Kid, they're waiting."

It wasn't Alex. Jack was the only one who called me Kid. I opened the door immediately. "Why are you doing this?"

"I want photos."

"But why?"

His expression hardened. He was never appreciative of anyone questioning his desires. "Because I want them.

Are we going to have a problem?"

No. No we weren't. I shook my head immediately, as Jack looked me over. "Perfect," he said, admiring me from all sides. "You look like a pinup."

He led me, keeping me steady in those crazy heels, down the hallway to the front entry, where the white backdrop was in place; the hot lights were on. "Samantha," he said, "this is my friend Rick. He shoots the most beautiful women in the world for some of the most prestigious magazines. And he lost a bet to me."

Rick actually smiled. "Your man knows how to bluff," he said before returning to his camera. "Are we ready?"

Jack echoed the query. "Are we, Sam? Are we ready?"

I took a deep breath and then let myself be positioned where they wanted me.

"We'll start slowly," Rick said, his voice kind. "A few test shots."

He had a Polaroid camera in hand—you remember Polaroids, don't you?—and he snapped a couple of pictures, and then took the time to let them develop before going over the shots with his assistants and Jack. I remained where I was, awkwardly posed, odd girl out. Heart racing so loud and fast I was sure the rest of the group could hear the sound.

Then Rick was back, his voice low, the way Jack's was when he truly wanted me to relax. Telling me that we were all friends here. That nobody was in a hurry. That we were going to have a little fun. His idea of fun, anyway. My idea of a waking nightmare.

Music came on then, one of Rick's assistants sliding a disc into place. And next the camera. Flashing. And flashing again.

"You're beautiful," Rick said, and I looked at him,

startled. Actually thinking of disagreeing. "You're beautiful," he said again, and I looked down, then back up, under my lashes as he took the picture.

I could feel Jack watching me. I could feel Jack wanting me to please him. Wanting me not to cross my arms over my body. Wanting me not to be nervous and shy. But those sensations warred within me.

I'm not a model, that voice in my head said. *I'm not beautiful*, it reminded me cruelly.

"This way," Rick said. "Give me that look again..."

Chapter Thirty-Three
A Picture of You

Jack was the one to offer a sip of whiskey. He poured a glass and brought it over, actually holding the drink to my lips and tipping to give me a taste of the fiery liquid. I'd done fine until now, trying my best to follow the photographer's detailed instructions, while also knowing not to fake too much. Everyone here grasped the fact that I wasn't a model. Nobody expected me to transform into one of those glamorous Amazons within a couple of hours.

But that didn't make taking my top off any easier.

This wasn't a pressure job. This was a Jack fantasy. And if I'd paid closer attention to our lunchtime exchange, I would have understood that he was preparing me then. That he was giving me the briefest taste of what he planned for the future.

Public exposure.

Which, at the moment, meant undoing the satin bra and letting the fabric fall open. Letting Rick catch me like that before pulling the bra all the way off.

"Cross your arms," Rick said, "and give me that look again. That pouty look. I love that."

"She does pout well, doesn't she?" Jack asked, sounding pleased, and in a way, sounding as if I weren't there at all. As if I couldn't hear.

Once again, I wished for my long hair back. I wished I could tilt my head and hide behind my bangs. But with my short cut, I was revealed. Shorn. No place to go. Rick took several pictures, with additional instructions, and then went to consult with Jack. I watched Alex talking with the assistants, and I was surprised when Rick joined their group, when his two flunkies left the room with Alex.

So now there were three of us: Jack, Rick, and me. And now I was starting to worry about the whiskey Jack kept bringing over. Little sips only. But sips for confidence, I could tell.

"You have to know what I want," he said softly while Rick was changing film—yes, this was back in the day of rolls of film—and I shook my head. I had no idea. But looking at him, I noticed that he was dressed different than he had been at lunch. He was in black slacks and a black long-sleeved sweater, and while he waited for me to understand, I watched Rick moving a chair onto the white sheet.

"Jack," I started, realization dawning. "Wait, Jack."

But there was no waiting now. There was only my man, with his strong hand on my wrist, dragging me toward that hard-backed chair. There was only Rick getting ready, maneuvering closer. There was only Jack, pulling me over his lap, and Rick taking the picture. Jack, sliding my panties down my thighs, and Rick catching the shot. Jack, lifting his hand and bringing his palm down hard on my naked ass, and Rick clicking his camera.

I understood now why they'd let the assistants go—probably out to the hot tub with Alex for a well-deserved soak. I understood that I'd been punished onstage before, in front of an audience, that this scene should be easy for me.

But it wasn't.

Jack spanked me hard, not seeming to want a true staged-for-camera shot. He spanked me over and over, and Rick was right there, chronicling each blow.

The whiskey had warmed me, but my heart still hammered.

"All right," Rick said after a moment, "you want to try the next shot?"

"Yeah," Jack agreed, "hand me the one on top."

I didn't turn my head fast enough to see what they were talking about. Didn't need to. The paddle came into play almost instantaneously, a painted wooden paddle from the feel of the powerful impact on my skin. I didn't cry out, but I sucked in my breath. Jack clearly had no intention of playing make-believe with the camera. He wanted an exhibition in reality. He wanted to see the tears streak down my face, wanted to see the cherry-hued flush to my naked ass.

Each time the paddle met my skin, I jumped. And each time the pain flared through me, the photographer took the picture. Rick was in constant motion, and I was never unaware of the fact that he was working through rolls of film. My face burned with embarrassment at first, then slowly, gradually, I had to stop thinking of the photo shoot aspect of the evening and concentrate on the spanking.

Day Six. A simple over-the-knee session with me sprawled across Jack's lap? Not really. I'd experienced far worse pain wise, but not much worse as far as my level of mortification. What would happen if Jack made me sob? What would Rick think of me? What did he think of me now? How close a friend was he to Jack? At night, did Rick spank one of his assistants? Were they buddies in pain, or only buddies in poker?

Jack didn't stop even after Rick assured him he'd gotten all of the shots. Jack continued, paddling me mercilessly until I kicked out, struggling in spite of the fact that I knew Rick was still watching us, desperate to behave, but unable to fulfill that desire.

"Spread your legs," Jack demanded, and I obeyed, my eyes shut now in anticipation. Jack dropped the paddle and used his bare hand, four fingers tight together as he spanked my pussy over and over. The fear of potential pain turned into a craving for future pleasure, and for the first time during the evening's events, I started to honestly relax, absorbing each blow, rocking on Jack's lap, now not caring at all about Rick, still taking pictures, still clicking away.

When I came, I saw lights. Flashes of pure molten silver in front of my eyes.

And then Jack was lifting me up and carrying me naked down the hall to the master bedroom, leaving everything else behind...

Chapter Thirty-Four: Seven

As you can imagine, the photo shoot had made me wet. Parading around in front of a trio strangers while wearing only the skimpiest of outfits was a surprise turn-on. But truly, being spanked for the camera was what excited me the most. And it wasn't just me. When Jack carried me back to the bedroom, he didn't even bother shutting the door. He was fucking me almost as soon as we reached the bed, only pausing to split open his slacks before sliding inside of me.

"You looked so amazing," he said as he drove forward, "in those sexy outfits."

"Yeah?" I wanted more.

"The way you stared at Rick. That expression in your eyes. Jesus," he said, "I could hardly wait. I wanted to fuck you out there. With the lights and the camera. I wanted to bend you over the chair and fuck the daylights out of you with everyone around, with all of those people watching. You would have let me, too. I know it. You would have loved every fucking second."

We were doing it missionary, the most standard sex position in the book, and yet we hardly ever found ourselves like this in bed, face to face, man on top. And when we did, it was rarely unfettered.

"I could tell how hard the experience was for you," Jack continued, his gaze locked on my face.

I nodded.

"Why?"

"The people..."

"You've been onstage," he reminded me.

Talking while fucking was so difficult. But Jack loved these types of Q and A sessions. The fact that his cock was working me throughout the whole conversation was like an added bonus for him. He loved to put me on edge, especially when I felt as if I might melt away to nothing in a matter of moments.

"I don't know," I started. "The lights and the assistants, and Rick."

"He's a professional."

"But he doesn't usually take pictures of women getting spanked like that, does he?"

"As a *fetish* photographer? Yeah, I think he's seen far worse. Or better."

Now Jack flipped me, taking me from behind so I could no longer see his eyes. A fetish photographer. That's not what he'd said before. If I'd known, would the shoot have been easier for me? Probably, but who can say? Jack's hands ran over my body, lingering on my still-smarting ass. He'd spanked me hard for the camera, not holding back at all, and I could still feel every stroke. Jack understood. He teased me, touched me, petted me until I was right on the cusp, and then he pulled out once more.

I sat up with the sheets all around me, trying to guess

what would happen next, but having no idea. My eyes wide, I watched while Jack stripped off his clothes, then climbed back on the bed. His body was warm and hard next to mine, and he gripped me by the nape of my neck and pushed me down, so that my mouth was poised right above his cock.

"Go on," he said, "you know what I want."

I licked slowly at first, tasting myself, the fragrant flavor of my juices. Then I hit the rhythm that Jack liked best, bobbing for him, swallowing him deeper down my throat with each motion. He trailed his fingertips along my spine, traced every one of my tattoos, before pulling me on top of him into a sixty-nine. Jack seemed to want to take things easy on me. I'd supposed he would give me another spanking back here in the privacy of the bedroom, but he made no move to get out any paddles or floggers, not even to reach for his belt. And soon I was lost in the pleasure of his mouth on my pussy and my own private mission to make him come.

But this position didn't mean Jack grew quiet. In between taps of his tongue on my clit, he continued to talk to me. "You pouted so pretty," he said, "so perfect. I can't wait to see what the pictures look like when Rick develops them."

I did my best not to grind myself against him. Every time he stopped with his tongue, I felt desperate. I wanted him to make me come. I wanted him to suck on my clit like it was a piece of hard candy.

"And, of course, we'll have to go a bit further next time."

Next time. That's what got me. The images appeared before my shut lids. What Jack might do. How he might want me. Jack held out until after the climax flooded through my body, twisting me and turning me inside out and back again. I didn't release my hold on his cock, though. I kept sucking and slurping him through my own pleasure, and then he bucked and came. Powerful. Silent. Lifting me up in the air, filling my mouth and my throat with the warm liquid of his release.

"What bet did Rick lose?" I managed to ask afterward, when we were wrapped up together under the blankets. Jack smiled at the question, and my heart raced. God, he was handsome. Sometimes I forgot to admire him, to appreciate the fine lines of his face, the shadows beneath his eyes.

"Simple poker game. Stakes got a little high and he was cash poor. I was the one to suggest this as a wager."

"What would he have gotten if *he'd* won?" I whispered, but Jack turned out the light and pulled me close. Not bothering to answer. Not giving me a clue. But I could imagine. My thoughts kept me awake long after I sensed my man had drifted to sleep.

In the morning, Jack went to the office even earlier than usual. He was logging in extraordinary hours in preparation for our trip—weekends, evenings, it didn't seem to matter. But he kissed me before departing and promised to do his best to be home at a decent hour.

"Decent," I repeated, mocking him.

"I'm only talking about the hour," he assured me, "nothing else."

I stayed in bed as long as I could, until I felt guilty for being so lazy. And then I showered and headed to the living room, where Alex was already waiting for me. Everything from the previous evening was gone, the house completely back to normal. Even the lingerie I'd worn, the various changes I'd slipped on and off throughout the evening, had all been put away. Alex's efficiency at work once more.

"You want to go back to Sunset?" he asked.

"Jack doesn't have plans for me?"

"I didn't say that."

I glared at him. Sometimes I found Alex's attitude amusing. Sometimes I wanted to smack him, to wrestle him to the ground, to overpower him with sheer will even if I didn't have the strength to make the vision come true.

"I'm ready," I told him, heading out the door to the car. On the front seat was a cream-colored envelope with my name written in Jack's handwriting. I didn't want to read the note while Alex watched, but there was no way I could wait until we'd arrived back home. Breathless, I broke the seal and pulled out the letter.

There was no note.

There were no photographs.

There was only a single word:

Seven.

Chapter Thirty-Five
The Number

Alex didn't ask me what the note said. And I didn't offer up any information. Of course, I couldn't guess what Jack meant by the single word—except perhaps a reminder, and that was unnecessary. I knew precisely what today was, what today meant.

We drove back to Sunset, and I was grateful when Alex dropped me off in front of the building. I wasn't in any sort of mood to hang out with the blond Dom-in-training. Instead, I relished spending the day almost entirely by myself. I took the time to write, to clean up, to choose an outfit of my own, without any hints. I knew better than to wear jeans or slacks. Not on a day when Jack planned to deliver the finale in the week dedicated to spankings. Pants would have been too in-your-face. A skirt was far more submissive.

Still, Jack hadn't told me whether we were going out or staying in. He hadn't said anything at all except that he'd be home early. So I was ready, and in case we were going out, I was fancy. And in case we were going out to a club, I was fetishy. And in case we were staying in, I had a glass of Jack's favorite whiskey poured and waiting.

But I was ready too early.

He'd said a decent hour. But he hadn't given a specific time. So I'd already drained the first glass and was a bit into the second when the door opened.

Jack came into the room with a bouquet of flowers. Seven red roses. He set them by my side, then lifted the drink from my hand, taking a sip before placing the glass on the edge of the table.

"You look lovely," he said, admiring my black vinyl outfit, shiny in the lights coming in from the window. "I knew you wouldn't let me down."

I felt a wave of pleasure spread through me. Obeying Jack's wishes when a verbal command hadn't even been given was one of my highest goals. I'm no mind reader, but I am observant.

"We're going out tonight," he said. "I'll get cleaned up, and then we'll leave."

I drank the rest of the whiskey while Jack dressed. My nerves were taut. The week had built up to this evening—and I had no idea what sort of explosive ending Jack might have planned. He reemerged in black, his go-to color, and then nodded to me. It was time to depart.

The drive surprised me. I'd thought we were going to Juliette's, but I was wrong. Jack took me instead to the gallery of Serafina, a woman I'd massaged in the not-so-distant past. This was simply one more instance of Jack's world and my world overlapping. The gallery had been bought for Serafina by her husband. This couple had their own unique relationship. Sera had been a topless dancer, and her man had fallen hard, then worked to recreate her, to transform her into someone who would be accepted by the high-end society in which he traveled. The gallery was his idea, and yet she constantly chose to feature the most avant-garde art, upsetting his careful plans. In my head, he couldn't have been that disappointed by her actions. He always seemed to be pleased by the excitement that swirled around her.

Tonight was an opening.

I knew I wasn't dressed correctly as soon as we walked in. And I knew that Jack didn't give a shit. He didn't mind if people stared at my far-too-short vinyl skirt with the chrome hardware, at my fishnet stockings, at the vinyl bustier that made the most of my small breasts. He didn't mind people gazing at my patent-leather Docs, at the collar on my throat, at the fact that Jack held me by my wrist far more often than he took me by the hand.

Basically, Jack didn't mind that I was as avant-garde in this crowd as the art on the walls. In fact, I could tell he liked the added attention I'd won for us. But I was blushing from the first step in the building.

The owner came forward as soon as she saw Jack. The two knew each other through her husband. Serafina greeted me courteously, as if I were a stranger, never indicating that I had seen her naked, that I had rubbed her body with scented oils and listened to her secrets. This was not the first time I'd received that sort of oddly stilted welcome. Even my former boss's mother, who I'd massaged on several occasions, treated me differently in social events. As if she knew me from long ago, but couldn't place my name. Doesn't bother me, but I am aware of the judgment. The upstairs/downstairs reactions of the rich: can't fraternize with the help.

When Serafina moved on to her other guests, I felt

more at ease. And as soon as Jack and I began to make our way through the gallery, a true peace began to steal over me. I was an art history major in school, and art has always relaxed me. Ultimately, I was able to ignore the whispers and focus on the pictures, showing Jack the ones I liked the best as we made our way from room to room, until we reached the smallest space at the back of the gallery.

"Here's what I wanted you to see," Jack said, and I walked with him around the final room.

There were seven pictures.

Seven color photographs.

Seven visions of a girl's body.

Seven images of me.

"Rick rushed them," Jack explained into my silence. "He's having a full exhibition here next month. "And Sera did me the favor, since she knew I'd buy the whole set."

I looked again at the first shot, the girl over the man's lap, panties still on, paddle in hand, the blur of dark hair, the feet in the air.

"Jack..."

"We were supposed to do the shoot earlier in the week," he continued, "but Rick's schedule was a nightmare. That's why these are small, unfinished..."

He stroked my ass through my skirt as he spoke, and although I knew that nobody in the room would guess that the model was me, or that the lap I was over was Jack's, I felt as exposed as if my driver's license had been blown up and framed as the last picture in the room.

The hipster set moved around us, drinking the free champagne, nibbling the gourmet appetizers that were passed around by actors pretending to be waiters (or vice versa). There was white noise in my head—I could hear the murmurs, the rumblings, but no clear words sounded in my ears. All I could do was stare at the pictures, feeling Jack's arm tighten around my waist, feeling his heat, his strength.

I was conflicted. I wanted to stay and look, to drink in the images. Muybridge had nothing on Rick. He'd captured art in motion. He'd captured the true emotion of being exposed. But the other part of me wanted to run and hide. Jack understood. He didn't waste time with small talk. He said our good-byes to the hostess, then laced his fingers with mine and led me from the gallery.

Seven flowers. Seven pictures. What did Jack have next on the agenda? I knew there would be something. But I had no idea...

Chapter Thirty-Six
Seven Sins

Can you name them? Care to try?

Greed.
Sloth.
Wrath.
Envy.
Gluttony.
Pride.
Lust.

Yes, I saved the best for last. Doesn't everyone do that?

Dinner was seven courses. I should have guessed, I suppose. Seven courses at one of the most exclusive restaurants in town. Sad to say that most of the places where we liked to go have long disappeared. Los Angeles diners are fickle like that. The hottest spots are no longer hot when everyone learns of their existence. But this was one of the places Jack liked best, where he and I could linger in a corner, where a waiter who knew us by first name would bring surprise treats from the kitchen.

Once we were seated, I was able to ward off my embarrassment at my vinyl attire simply by focusing on Jack. Because over dinner, my man started to explain. "I enjoyed this week," he said. "Playing with you. Planning for you. The idea came from the photo shoot, and I choreographed everything around that concept."

He took his time describing the work that had gone into the week. As he spoke, I tasted each of the delicious dishes, but was in no mood to dally. I wanted to know what else Jack had up his sleeve. I wanted him to reveal the secrets to me. Because when I looked in his eyes, I saw that he was hiding something.

"And then tonight, I decided to plan something extreme," he continued. "Something magical to play on the seven-day theme, and I thought of the sins."

"Sins," I echoed.

"The seven deadly sins. Can you name them?"

I tried, missing only pride. Jack smiled at me when I counted each one off on my fingers. He said, "Sloth was letting you laze around all day. Gluttony was this meal. Pride was showing you the photos on display."

I sat there in semi-shock. How could Jack create situations like this? I mean, how could his mind work like this? He was so busy at the firm, and preparing for our trip. How was there any time—or energy—left for him to come up with such intricate plans?

When I asked, stammering over the question, he said, "This is what relaxes me. It's what gives me the most pleasure."

He took me back home afterward and opened the door slowly. Alex had been busy during our absence. I understood that right away. Jack's sex elf had created quite the homecoming display—on the table were seven boxes, and when I walked closer I saw that each one was numbered. Jack motioned for me to start with the first. "Sin number four," he said, smiling at me. "You do want them all, don't you, greedy girl?"

I nodded, mentally trying to figure out where we were, which sins were left: Wrath. Envy. Lust.

The first box contained a blindfold. The second wrist cuffs. The third ankle cuffs. The fourth held a gag. The fifth a vibrating egg. The sixth a paddle. The seventh a crop.

When I was surrounded by a mass of colored tissue paper and the wreckage of opened boxes, Jack instructed me to take off my clothes. Nervously, I skinned out of the vinyl outfit, then waited to see if he wanted me naked. Yes. So off came the panties and stockings, until I was stripped bare.

Jack helped me carry the new toys back to our bedroom, my hands overflowing with the kinky devices. Each one was expensive, I could tell from the way the toys and tools felt in my hands. Fine leather for the cuffs. Luxurious black velvet for the blindfold. Nothing tacky—not for Jack—but everything sexy. The whole time Jack was binding me down, using the new toys, I kept running over the remaining sins in my mind. I understood lust. I reveled in lust. But what did Jack expect me to be envious of, and what could he do that would possibly make me angry? More important than how was the question that rose up immediately—for what purpose would he want to push on that button?

The cuffs were tight but comfortable, and in minutes I was captured face down on our bed. Still my mind couldn't keep up with Jack's. Even though I consider myself to be a clever writer, my dangerous Dom always seemed able to out plan me, to surpass my most creative concepts. Suddenly, I heard footsteps from down the hall and saw Alex enter the room. And then, I thought I understood.

Jack fit the gag between my lips—oh, the hated, hateful gag—as Alex wrapped his arms around Jack's waist from behind. Anger flared through me. Why? I had no idea. Perhaps, it was because Alex had been in on the game from the start, helping to plan, while I'd been kept in the dark. Or maybe it was simply the fact that he was free while I was bound. Even though I live for bondage, for being tied and kept in one place, that didn't change the fact that Alex was able to run his hands along Jack's body, to kiss the back of Jack's neck. That's exactly when the bitch named Envy kicked in. Because Jack turned and gripped the back of Alex's hair tightly, and he returned the kiss with passion.

Anger and envy warred within me.

Who was I angry at? For some reason, I focused my wrath upon Alex. Even though Jack was the one who planned the event. Even though Jack was the one responsible for every step of this carefully scheduled evening. Maybe I was too in love to be angry at my Dom.

Before I could think, Jack turned his attention on me. He seemed to understand all of the crazy thoughts spiraling in my head. His eyes glittered in the light, animal eyes, when he picked up the blindfold.

I shook my head. I tried to pull away. To no avail. I was bound as tight as I could possibly be. Jack had seen to that. There was no escape. The blindfold slipped over my eyes, plunging me into darkness. But Jack was not through with me. In seconds, I felt his fingertips between my thighs, and then I heard his laugh.

"You're wet," he said. "Your body never lies, Sam. Your mind tells you one thing, but your cunt tells me something else."

I bit down on the gag in my mouth, bitter tasting, foul.

Jack slid the vibrating egg inside of me, and in seconds, the pulses spread through me, radiating outward to the very tips of my fingers. Jack was right. I couldn't fight with the pleasure flowing through me, couldn't fight with this sensation. But in my head, visions of Alex and Jack, of what they might be doing, continued to play. A mental blue movie running endlessly through my mind...

Chapter Thirty-Seven
A Question of Lust

Dreams blur with fantasies for insomniacs like me. The past dances with the present. When I have a difficult time sleeping, I add to the confusion. Rather than wait until the proper time to get out of bed, I'll brew the coffee at a quarter past three. Mug in hand, silk black sky out my windows, I'll feel as if I could be anywhere. Sitting at a hotel desk in Vienna. Working in a friend's apartment in Paris. And it could be anytime. Late in the evening. Early in the morning.

It's a blur.

But that night, there was no confusion. That night, life was diamond sharp. So clear. So precise. Every action counted. Every moment resonated.

Jack knew me intrinsically. He knew that *not* seeing was far worse than seeing. Years ago I read *Danse Macabre*, Stephen King's nonfiction book on horror, and I recall that King said the monster is always more terrifying while it's still behind the door. Because the reader pictures his or her own private horror. The revelation is never quite as awesome—or terrifying—as what was imagined.

Was this the same for me?

Blindfolded on the bed, imagining what Alex was doing to Jack or what Jack was doing to Alex. Lost from the start in the kiss that they'd shared. I felt as if every time I began to grow comfortable with our unique situation, something would happen to shake me up once more. Yet this was Jack. This was who he was. What he wanted. A duo of lovers. Or pets. Or slaves. Or subs.

Who was I to argue with that?

What Jack was to me went beyond boyfriend. Beyond lover. Beyond any of the simple words used to describe partners in the pain/pleasure world we shared. He understood our bond better than I did. Was that why he'd chosen to play out the seven deadly sins? To take me on a tour through the very depths of my emotions?

Anger and lust and envy. Why did they go so well together? Why did my heart beat so damn hard at the thought of him kissing Alex? Stripping Alex. Fucking Alex.

I wasn't entirely forced into sensory deprivation. I could hear. I knew when Jack told Alex to take off his clothes. I knew when Jack bound Alex to the chair against the wall, handcuffs on his wrists, leather thongs on his ankles. Now I was confused.

Who was the plaything this evening? Was it going to be Alex? Who was the voyeur, and who was the exhibited?

"Day Seven," Jack said, surprising me with his proximity. My ears were playing tricks on me. "You're ready? You've been waiting?"

I couldn't speak, but I nodded.

"We'll use your new toy first," he told me, and then I

heard the rush of the paddle in the air, felt the slam of the lacquered wood against my bare skin. The vibrator was still rumbling away within me, but on a setting far too low to get me off. Still that dangerous combo of pleasure-tinged pain had me straining uselessly against Jack's bindings. I thought of Alex watching. I thought of Jack gazing down at me, deciding how long to wait before striking the next blow. How much I could take? Jack knew full well what the downtime would mean to me.

And it meant this... As soon as my body absorbed the shock, I needed more. Raising up, begging silently. As soon as he paddled me again, I retreated, thinking that I didn't want this punishment. Didn't require any additional torment. Until, bizarre as the thought might seem, my body proved me wrong.

Harder, my mind cried out. *Harder, Jack, please...*

He gave me ten. Only ten. A twisted teaser. Not enough for tears even. Not enough to bring me to the brink. Then he walked away from the bed. I heard him talking to Alex, whispering, his words too low for me to make out. And then I heard Alex groan. Not seeing—was it worse, as King suggested? Did I imagine fantasies far more decadent than what was actually occurring? Had Jack put nipple clamps on Alex, or was he firmly stroking his cock in one fist while describing Alex's future. Had he lit candles to tip over Alex's naked skin, or was he merely promising to do to his assistant all the dreamy actions he was currently doing to me?

The gag was awkward, but I found relief in not having a chance to speak. If he'd taken out the red rubber ball from between my lips, would I have been begging, or yelling? Would I denounce Jack as a bastard, or coo that he was my Master? My emotions took me for a wild ride, but I realized simply that Jack had saved me. Saved me from having to worry...there was no chance to get myself in trouble with my mouth. He'd taken away that possibility. Removed the very concept from the start.

Alex groaned again, an erotic sound, not of pain at all, but of pleasure. Oh, Jesus, what was Jack doing to him? Flickers of X-rated images played before my shut eyes, and I was so focused on the vision that once again I missed Jack's footsteps returning to the bed. Missed my warning before he pulled out the vibrating egg with a vicious tug and left me empty and shaking. I knew what was next. The crop was next.

Anger had disappeared. Envy was gone.

Left for me was only lust.

Chapter Thirty-Eight
In My Shoes

Put yourself in my place. Bound to the bed, waiting for pain, but anticipating pleasure. Or waiting for pleasure, but anticipating pain. The two are tightly linked together for me in so many ways. Or perhaps one begets the next. By this point, I am beyond feeling guilty for my desires, and yet I still manage to be ashamed of them.

Does that make sense?

I adore women who are up front with their sexuality. Who grab their desires by the neck and claim each one in a loud, proud voice. I know women like that. I'm friends with some, in awe of others. And yet I don't think I will ever get over the shame of my own turn-ons, because I don't truly want to. The shame is part of the pleasure for me. The dark, dirty sensations that slide over me, the chill that runs through me. I can't imagine having my desires spread out in a clean, well-lit room where everyone can conclude that they are healthy and normal and delightful.

I don't want to be absolved for my sins.

Especially, not lust.

Jack understood that part of me. He knew when he reached for a crop that I was cringing inside. Not so much because I could envision the future medley of marks that would decorate my pale skin. But because I wanted that undeniable pain just as much as I was afraid of it. Maybe more.

I wanted him to make me burn.

On this night, the crop was next. The crop was fierce. But my mind was still playing tricks on me. I knew Jack wasn't going to let me off easy—because this was Day Seven. This was the end of his game. I also knew that the cropping wasn't the finale. Not with Alex captured in a nearby chair. There would be no quick cropping and then curtains down. Jack had more planned. More and more and more.

But I needed to get through the punishment. And Jack was in a mood. The fact that he had so fully deprived me of my faculties told me that. I will say again how much I adore being bound. Just looking at the various bindings on X-rated websites has me shifting in my chair. But I have to add that the blindfold and gag freaked me out a bit. Once, for a short-lived magazine, I did a bit of research on sensory deprivation tanks. You would think I'd have loved the experience based on my kinks—but I despised every moment. That was a whole different game to me than cuffs or thongs or chains. That was my own private hell, and I could not wait to get out of the confining compartment. Now, with my sight gone and with my ability to beg taken away, I felt more vulnerable, which is how Jack wanted me.

He started slow. He let me grow accustomed to the rhythm and the weight of the tool on my naked skin, and then he lined up five blistering strokes in a row. Not being told to count was frightening because there was no gold ring to grasp, no final number to strive for. Not having an ability to speak was terrifying, even if I'd never tell Jack to stop—or at least, never mean the word *stop*. The gag became my focal point. I wished desperately that he'd remove the rubbery red ball. That orb between my lips made me feel ugly. I knew that Jack had a different perspective about the toy. He loved the way the red rubber ball stretched my lips open. He loved the fact that I couldn't bite on my bottom lip, couldn't worry it between my teeth, couldn't give in to any of the tics I'm accustomed to.

As the pain flared through me, my eyes started to tear. I was going to wet the blindfold, I thought, and then, when Jack dropped the crop and touched my cunt, I thought: I am going to wet the bed. Wet the mattress with the juices coating my pussy lips. Jack said the words often enough to me: your body doesn't lie. I was starting to understand. Starting to accept. Accept the fact that one of the main reasons I was so damn excited was that Alex was in the room, too. Alex was watching.

Crazy that I had gotten to this point in only a few months. Crazy, in some ways, that a sweet girl like me, who'd been steps from the aisle, had wound up in a topsy-turvy three-way relationship. Where nothing ever was what it seemed. I could have been married by now, and on the way to being one of the cookie-cutter wives who talked of nothing but curtains and Pilates. Who wore beige. Who drove a Volvo.

And instead, instead of the glamorous two-hundred-person wedding at the estate owned by Byron's father, instead of the honeymoon in Hawaii and the regrets that would have draped over me for the rest of my life, I was tied to a bed by a man I'd have done anything for, being watched by another who I believed felt the same way. The same way about Jack.

When *he* was done—and not one stroke earlier—Jack dropped the crop, and I heard his footsteps on the floor. He was moving to Alex. He was going to play with him now. I wondered, somewhere deep in my psyche, whether Jack had been choreographing a similar sort of game with Alex. Had his assistant been on the receiving end of seven days of pain, as well? Or was this some reward of a different type?

I wished the blindfold were off. Wished I could see. Instead, I strained my ears to hear Jack murmuring to Alex. Listened hard to the moans Alex made. Was Jack touching him, or teasing him? Was Alex begging...why did that thought make me even wetter?

"It's a choice," Jack said, and I think I stopped breathing for a moment to try to make out Alex's response. "A simple choice," Jack said again.

Knowing Jack, understanding how carefully he planned every action, I realized that there was more. Perhaps the end of Day Seven was rapidly approaching, but the game was far from over.

Chapter Thirty-Nine
Love's Language

Pity isn't one of the seven deadly sins, but that was the best emotion to describe me at the moment. Waves of self-pity began to replace those waves of lust.

For several minutes, I was entirely still, my whole body tensed, simply listening. I couldn't figure out what was going on in the corner of the room. And although I was desperate to ask, desperate to know, my ability to speak had been removed. So there I was, both captive and captivated, yearning for some clue, craving some sign.

It was as if Jack had forgotten all about me.

Sad little sub on the bed, I was, my mind running fast while my body was held in place. I couldn't stop the questions tearing through my brain:

Why was Jack ignoring me?

What could he be doing to Alex?

And more selfish than that—wasn't Day Seven supposed to be about *me*? *My* fantasies? *My* desires?

There was no reason for me to think that. Yet I did. I

wallowed in the emptiness left by Jack's departure, even though he'd only taken several steps away from the bed. I agonized in the bindings, the blindfold, the gag. A chill crept over me, and I began making up horror stories in my mind. Jack leaving me like this for the rest of the night. Jack refusing to return to the mattress, intent on taking care of Alex instead of me.

Loving Alex instead of me.

Quickly, envy approached once more. If I'd been part chameleon, my skin would have turned a shimmering emerald green.

Until finally, dear god, finally, I heard footsteps. Jack was at my side, and he was laughing. "Leave you alone for two fucking seconds, and you implode, don't you?" he said, stroking my hair, tugging on the short strands. "You go too deep inside of yourself, and you tell yourself all sorts of dangerous lies. Isn't that true?"

I nodded. He had me pegged.

"There's more than enough here," he continued, "for both of you."

The fortune cookie moral for the day.

"You understand that, don't you? You can grasp that concept, right?"

His fingers undid the ball gag as he spoke, so that I could swallow again, press my face against the bed and wipe my cheeks. Lick my lips in that nervous way of mine. I waited, head up next, to see if he would remove the blindfold, but he didn't.

"There is no end," he continued, "does that make sense?"

I wished I could see his eyes. I wanted to know what he was referring to. No end to the pain of the evening. No end to his ability to torture. No end to Day Seven.

Or no end to his ability to juggle the two of us—me and Alex—our different personalities, our completely unique emotions. I had the feeling that Jack was trying to reach me somehow. To show me, to explain. And yet although he had a better mastery of words than I did—verbally, anyway—he was being purposefully vague. That was the only explanation I could come up with. Until he removed the blindfold and turned my head, and I could see that Alex had been placed in a similar position to my own. Yes, he was upright, bound to the chair, but he had a bright red ball gag in place between his full lips, and he had a black velvet blindfold on, and he was—as far as I could tell—my other half. My male twin.

Jack climbed onto the bed with me. He pressed down on me with his fully clothed body, letting me feel his weight against me. Letting me experience how hard he was.

"Can you see?" he whispered. "Can you see what I like?"

I had thought I knew. I'd thought I understood.

"The mess of it," he continued, his voice so damn whiskey-smooth. "The sensation of playing with a heat others fear. A heat so intense that someone, without a doubt, someone will be burned." Alex's head was turned to us, and I knew he was listening, straining, the way I had. What was Jack talking about, though? Why couldn't he speak more plainly for me?

"We came apart for a little while," Jack continued, "so you had me to yourself. All to yourself. And I reveled in that. But I need this. I can't tell you how often. I can't explain why. But I do. The whole package." He paused, then repeated again, "The whole fucking mess of it. I don't want neat and orderly. I have that in my job. I must have it for my work. After hours, I want something else. Something electrifying. Something that makes me feel alive."

And there was Alex, bound like a statue, so still, his muscular chest moving only in breath. His thighs spread apart, ankles bound to the chair. He looked like an X-rated version of *The Thinker.* He looked like a statue come to life, or an artist's model waiting to be captured as a statue. Immortalized.

I stared at him, and then looked over my other shoulder, wanting to meet Jack's eyes. Wanting to see the blue, the true color that would make me relax. Questions ricocheted in my brain. But I couldn't manage to speak.

"It isn't simple," he said, still not moving into my line of vision, keeping himself behind me. "I understand that. Our relationship is not normal. It's not safe. And yet, I'm asking you—I'm telling you what I need—I'm asking you once more whether you can handle the concept. Whether you can try."

Normal. What is normal anyway? I didn't need normal, but I wanted safe. I wanted to see Jack's eyes.

He seemed finally to realize, and he moved next to me on the bed, cradled my chin in his hand, said the words he only rarely spoke. Not every day. Not every week. But when I truly needed to hear them.

He said, "I love you."

And I said, "Yes."

Chapter Forty
Need You Tonight

I think it was that word, and the way Jack said the word, that changed me. Before, Jack had focused on what the word *need* meant to me. Back at the very beginning... "Don't worry so much because I need this, too."

But we'd been talking about my needs. My twisted cravings. He had been intent on reassuring me, soothing me in the safety, promising that he wouldn't run from what I dreamed about. This night was different. Even if Alex and I were the ones bound and helpless, this night was all about Jack.

My blue-eyed man didn't reveal weaknesses very often. He didn't pull back the scarlet rippling velvet and let me see the man behind the curtains. Not unless he had something serious to say, serious to share. Otherwise, the things he did, the way we played, these were all performed in a matter-of-fact sort of way. No matter how kinky. No matter how fucking deviant.

But when he whispered the simple statement to me—"I

need this"—and when he continued, not going in the direction I would have thought... *because I'm into men, because I'm bi*, any of those explanations, but because it was the chaos, the intricate web caused by the fact that he wanted not one lover but two. And not some meek sort of lovers, but people like Alex and myself, who might be led along, but who would rebel. Who might willingly follow, but who would also dig in our heels and question... Demand reassurance. Fuck up his plans. Things started to make sense to me. Things started to get clearer.

Need.

I still think of that concept all the time. Pops up whenever I hear the Stones song. When I was with Byron I fooled myself—or drugged myself—into thinking that I could get by with what we did. Because I believed at the time that the cravings I had were all about wants. I drank the Kool-Aid for as long as I possibly could. It took the breakup, took meeting Connor and then Nate and then Jack for me to determine that I wasn't really looking for wants. I was interested in finding what I needed. Without having those needs filled, I was the girl in the mini silver car who kept thinking of turning the wheel hard into an overpass wall. I was the girl who would forget to eat for a few days at a time because my stomach was so constantly tied up in knots. I was the girl who behaved in reckless, unsafe ways because I just didn't fucking care anymore. The pain of life was too obliterating.

Jack gave me everything I needed. Everything I'd always known I needed, but I'd tamped down, buried underground. And he took me beyond the fantasies I'd allowed myself into a whole new world. Who was I to deny him the same sensations? If he needed Alex, then shouldn't I shove over on the bed and make room for the boy? If he needed the two of us to be there for him, when he called, at his desire, then shouldn't I get over the rage and envy and floods of emotions that Alex brought up in me?

As you might imagine, it's not a yes or no answer.

Yes, I'd agree to what Jack was asking. I'd be part of the tangle. But no, I couldn't simply turn off the way Alex made me feel. Yet I didn't think Jack really wanted me to. He didn't expect to find me and Alex curled up together like kittens on the sofa, giving each other tongue baths in our off time. I believe that he appreciated the friction between us. That he used that very heat to his own advantage.

Like now, when he unbuckled the cuffs from my wrists, undid the thongs on my ankles, and had me stand. I was shaky as I waited to see what he had in mind next. I started to catch on when he performed the same tricks on Alex's bindings, and then led Alex, still blindfolded, to the bed. While I watched, he bound Alex in my place and then, without a word, he bound me in Alex's. Sitting me down on the hard wood chair. Letting me know that I would be the one to watch, and Alex would be the one to receive his attentions.

Alex was nervous. I could tell. His body—that fine, tight muscular body—was stiff with the worries that flickered through him. But he was in the spotlight, and I could also tell how much he enjoyed that, could tell by the way he shifted his hips that he was searching for exactly the right friction against the mattress. I knew what that felt like. The quiet attempt to get off with the precise pressure, to sneak out a little pleasure before Jack could intervene.

Jack slapped his ass for the attempt, even if Alex hadn't been seriously trying to come. There was more to this evening's events than for me to watch Alex cream against the sheets. Even I understood that, and Alex had been with Jack for far longer than I had.

Once Jack started, I felt as if I were watching a film I'd already seen. But one I couldn't quite remember. Because instead of the main character being me—the star was Alex. Yet Jack performed quite the same way with the boy that he had with me. There was the vibrating egg, this time lubed up and slipped between Alex's rear cheeks and into his asshole, eliciting a moan that made my mouth go dry. There was the paddle, hard and firm against Alex's hindquarters until they turned a rosy pink. And then there was the crop, slicing through the air, decorating Alex's ass with the stripes that I had on my own derriere, stripes that made sitting up so straight and firm more painful than I let on with my posture alone.

Each time the pain flared through Alex, I felt a mirroring emotion ripple through me. I wasn't sorry for Alex. But I knew what he was going through. I could relate, even if I couldn't quite sympathize. I didn't want to feel for him. I couldn't muster the emotion.

Jack didn't speak to Alex as he put him through the paces. But I could tell that the evening was getting to my handsome Dom. He stripped off his shirt, so that he was bare-chested, and I watched through half-shut lids as he punished his assistant. I would have squeezed my thighs together, dripping wet as I was, but Jack had bound me with my legs apart. Knowing, of course knowing what this moving picture would do to me.

While I watched Jack, I wondered what sorts of thoughts were running through his head. He was the scriptwriter of our sensual scenario. He was Atlas, and he held up our world on his strong, capable shoulders.

I felt as if Jack were merely priming Alex the way he had prepared me. The question in my mind was: What for? What was next?

I had no idea. But I could guess. And I could hope...

Chapter Forty-One
Shallow

All right, so I'm shallow. But I see sex everywhere I go.

I see sex in shoes and in clothes. In perfume and makeup. It's in my writing even when I am not penning porn. Sex is my sixth sense.

Others recognize this current running in me. Since I was fairly young, people have spilled their sexual secrets to me. Even when I was a virgin, the handsome, popular editor of our newspaper used to take me up to the tower building on campus and discuss his erotic encounters. More than simply bragging about conquests, Lance would describe the situations, the way he felt before, how he felt after. I was honored that he chose me as his confidante. I drank up every story he shared.

When I worked on an entertainment weekly, I developed an almost identical relationship with my managing editor (what is it about writers and their editors?), a man who had no idea how kinky I truly was, but who liked to see me blush. And, baby, do I blush. Over long lunches, he would describe how he'd held a woman down, stretching her body out with her wrists over her head. He would lower his voice and discuss exactly how he felt when he used a set of handcuffs on a girl for the very first time.

Bare acquaintances have bragged of their best nights.

Near strangers have shared secrets with me at bars.

There is something in my very personality that draws out exotic confessions from other people. I don't know if that's weird or not. But I adore secrets. I want to know all.

And this is what I've learned: If you're lucky, fucking transcends the actual motions. If you're truly blessed, then sex isn't even about the physical act. My editor knew that way back when. For him, sex was summed up by the way a girl looked at him before—and the way she looked after. For my editor in college, sex was a power play, and he had to come out on top. He wasn't into BDSM, but he was a top.

For Jack...for Jack I think sex was a tool. Sometimes a weapon of torture, sometimes an implement of almost unbelievable pleasure, but mostly a tool to slide inside the heads of his lovers. To open them up to him. Jack wanted to see how far he could go. To see how much we could take. How deep we would let him in.

Physical pain isn't ever as difficult for me to bear as emotional torment. Jack demolished my inner barriers, and that left me with far deeper scars than any welts he could cut into my skin.

This night, this seemingly endless night, was one of those times when Jack was testing. When he was seeing how willing we were to be led by him. Would he bring us to a place where we would cry out "No"? And if we actually dared to let that word slip from our lips, did we think he would actually stop?

There was no talk of safewords here.

I was still bound to the chair, watching, when Jack began to undress. I was frozen as he took off his clothes, as he pulled that vibrating toy from Alex's ass, as he positioned himself on the mattress. I was immobile as he lubed himself up, as he jerked his hand on his hard, strong cock—a vision that sent a tremor through me that made the wooden legs of the chair skitter on the floor—then spread apart Alex's fine rear cheeks. The last time this had happened, Alex had been dressed up like a doll, and I'd had a vibrant cobalt-blue strap-on in place. This time, I was a captive audience member, and Jack was just fucking. That's what it seemed like to me. There was no story to go along with this scene. There was only Jack, choosing a hole, taking what was rightfully his.

But I knew that I was meant to learn a lesson. I knew that Jack was trying to teach me something. There was never a time when we simply had sex. That's what I was trying to say before. With Byron, sex was sex. A pinpoint of pleasure (for him, anyway) in the dull daily routine of our miserable fucking lives. (Oh, how happy I am that I escaped.) But with Jack, sex was almost anything but the purely physical action of the quest for orgasm. Sex equaled power and lust and heartbreak and rules. Sex was a key to unlock a confession, a pleasure to withhold, a fantasy to strive for.

Jack pulled off Alex's blindfold as he fucked him, and I saw Alex blink in the light and watched him try his best to retain some semblance of self-control. But he had none. The cropping had raised mean welts on his skin. His eyes shone with tears. His mouth was still stretched by that hideous gag. As Jack rocked forward and back, he unbuckled the gag and dropped the thing to the floor. Now, Alex looked less frightened, more like himself. He stretched his mouth and licked his lips, and I mindlessly echoed the action, licking my own lips (you're doing it now, too, aren't you?), aware that I was imagining every sensation Alex was experiencing.

I'd been there. I'd done that.

I knew full well what it felt like to have Jack fuck me in this manner. I knew all about the rough ride of his cock in my asshole, the way I felt when he carried me to the point where I could come from this action alone. When Alex turned his head and saw me staring, he frowned. He never wanted me to see him in a position of weakness. He thought of himself as a Dom. Dom-in-Training, perhaps, but a Dom. To have me watch him stripped to this base place was the most difficult part of the evening for him. I could tell. He was like me in the precise, heady way he accepted pain. But embarrassment, awkwardness, ugliness, those concepts were far more difficult for him to bear. And Jack knew. Jack used our weaknesses the way a gambler uses a hidden ace.

Watching Jack move, I could tell he was far from climax. He didn't even seem to be putting his heart into the motions. He was fucking Alex to truly fuck him. To ream him. He was teaching Alex something as well. What? I couldn't tell. I wasn't part of their equation. I wondered once more whether Alex had been privately experiencing some form of seven days of sin the way I had. Was this his culmination? Was this his own pinnacle?

After several more thrusts, Jack pulled out and slipped his boxers back on. He came for me then. He undid my bindings, lifted me to standing, spread my thighs. He went on his knees before me, surprising me, and he parted the shaved lips of my pussy and touched my clit with his tongue. I was so dreamily wet, and he knew instantly that regardless of what I might say, or what I might think, I was fully turned on by his actions. By what he was doing to me, and what he was doing to Alex.

Slowly, he worked me, tongue slipping over my clit, then around in circles. Slowly, he teased me, and I kept my eyes shut tight, knowing Alex was watching. Knowing this was Alex's turn to feel envy. When Jack spun me around, I held on to the back of the chair, not having any idea what was in store for me, but trusting Jack thoroughly.

Was *that* tonight's lesson? Trust? I didn't think so.

I think Jack was showing us that he could see inside of us. That he could guess what we wanted, understanding even things we didn't know we craved. Displaying those yearnings for us. Making those fantasies come true.

Because deep down, didn't I *want* to see him top Alex? Deep down, in a place that I wouldn't visit myself without being forced there by Jack, didn't I relish watching him fuck someone else? Didn't I cream to see the way he treated Alex, roughly, manhandling him, taunting him?

Yes.

The answer to all of those questions is yes. Whispered in a sigh. Shouted out in an orgasmic scream. Yes, Jack. Yes!

Jack stayed on the floor, spread my own cheeks apart, and licked me there. My knees went weak at the pleasure. Jack pressed his face against me, driving his tongue inside of me, and I came for the first time of the evening. Came so hard that I moaned. Came so sweetly that I heard Alex echo my cry on the bed, a sound that made Jack pull back and laugh.

He'd gotten what he wanted. He'd shown us that we were connected. A fucked-up trio of desperate creatures. But one with invisible ties and bindings that were as strong as the physical cuffs he used to keep us in our place.

Chapter Forty-Two
And After

Nights when Jack shared his bed with the two of us were almost always like this. Not merely electric, but engulfed in flames. So often he played us against each other. Or took care of us first one and then the other. But when we all met on the mattress, when we all joined together—then I could truly understand what Jack wanted. The madness of the three of us. The tangle. The chaos.

I was made for ménages in so many ways. Although I am fiercely jealous, and endlessly possessive, I also am sexually demolished by the thought of overlapping limbs. At the sensation of being stroked and touched and embraced and caressed and adored by more than one lover at a time. My night with Ava and her roommate. My tequila-drenched experience with my two college buddies. Those experiences barely managed to prep me for what life would be like with a man like Jack.

That's a fallacy. Nothing really could have prepared me at all. Little girls aren't raised to want two grooms.

Barbie comes with Ken. Not Ken and Kirk. But my fantasies, though warped, were nothing compared to Jack's. To his daydreams. To his darkest desires.

Jack let me come one time, and then he led me to the bed. He wasn't done with his directing. How had we managed ourselves the previous time? With me the powerful current running between my two lovers. With my men book-ending me.

But tonight was different. Tonight, Alex was the spread. Tonight, Jack undid his bindings and let him free, then set us how he wanted us, with me on the bottom, and Alex next. Alex on top of me, not even needing to be told, although Jack said the words anyway.

"I want to watch."

I gazed at him, swallowing hard.

"Alex, I want to watch."

That's all he had to hear. In moments, Alex was grinding forward. Alex craving relief, release, any sort of pleasure to take the edge off what he'd been through. Jack stood by the bed for a moment, touching us both. His fingertips lingering on my lower lip, stroking through Alex's hair. He couldn't keep his hands off. I could hardly breathe, locking eyes with Jack as Alex plunged into me, my most recent climax still sending sparks throughout my body.

Jack watched, and he sighed, and then, when he couldn't wait any longer, he slid off his boxers and climbed back onto the mattress. I didn't have to look around to know what he was doing, where he was going. Jack took his spot back behind his boy, with one strong arm around Alex to hold him in place, impaling him once more.

I winced at the sensation as if I were the one being

pierced, feeling Alex freeze in place, then continue, more frantically, bucking inside of me.

"Oh, god, Jack, oh fucking god." Who'd said it? I don't know. It could have been me. It could have been Alex.

"Jesus, Jack."

Definitely Alex.

I knew what was going on. Couldn't pretend I didn't. But did I care? That's what Jack kept trying to get at. That's what he kept pressing on. Did I care? Could I live with the overlap? With the fact that he loved me, but he needed Alex. That he needed me, but he loved Alex. That there was no clean end in sight. No white wedding dress, unless Alex wore it half the night. No fancy honeymoon, unless Alex lay on the foot of the bed, his body so close we could reach out and touch him when we wanted to.

I'd recently escaped from a place where normal was the goal. Where gold-embossed Hallmark cards were read aloud as part of the entertainment at every birthday party. Jack seemed to understand instinctively that although I was so willing to be tamed, to be bent, to be led, I was also holding tight to some semblance of the real world. Of what normal people do. Of what they want. What they desire. And he wanted reassurance from me. He wanted to know if I was willing to forgo normal in favor of satisfaction. In favor of being fulfilled.

With Byron, my closet held expensive outfits in camel, navy, black.

In my new world, my closet was filled with vinyl.

With Byron, jewelry arrived on every birthday.

In my new world, a collar was as common as a necklace.

But most importantly, in my new world, the man I lived with—and lived for—needed more than I could be. I could go to the gym daily, I could cut my hair every which way, I could sport a realistic sex toy, but I'd never turn myself into a boy. Jack needed the man who was fucking me. He needed to inflict pain on us, exactly as much as we needed him to do precisely that.

Who was I to deny him his wishes?

Who was I not to give him everything I could?

Who was I?

Alex climaxed first, locked between us, fucking me so fiercely and fast that I could hardly react. I could feel the hot liquid inside me, could feel the way he trembled as the bliss flared through him. I came next, unable to stave off the pleasure any longer, my hand slipping between my thighs to stroke my clit just right. And then Jack, groaning, arching, thrusting so fucking hard that the whole bed shook.

Or the earth shook.

And after...after the shower. After the whiskey. After we were all cleaned up and relaxed in the living room, two on the sofa, one in the chair. After, there was peace among us.

And after that...there was Paris.

About the Author

Called "a trollop with a laptop" by *East Bay Express,* "a literary siren" by Good Vibrations and "the mistress of literary erotica" by Violet Blue, Alison Tyler is naughty and she knows it.

Over the past two decades, Ms. Tyler has written more than twenty-five explicit novels, including *Dark Secret Love*, *The Delicious Torment*, and *Tiffany Twisted*. Her novels and short stories have been translated into Japanese, Dutch, German, Italian, Norwegian, Spanish and Greek. When not writing sultry short stories, she edits erotic anthologies, including *Sudden Sex*, *The Big Book of Bondage*, *Kiss My Ass*, *Cuffed*, and *Bound for Trouble.* She is also the author of several novellas including *Cuffing Kate*, *Giving In*, *Banging Rebecca*, and *Those Girls.*

Ms. Tyler is loyal to coffee (black), lipstick (red), and tequila (straight). She has tattoos, but no piercings; a wicked tongue, but a quick smile; and bittersweet memories, but no regrets. She believes it won't rain if she doesn't bring an umbrella, prefers hot and dry to cold and wet, and loves to spout her favorite motto: *You can sleep when you're dead.* She chooses Led Zeppelin over the Beatles, the Cure over NIN, and the Stones over everyone. Yet although she appreciates good rock, she has a pitiful weakness for '80s hair bands.

In all things important, she remains faithful to her partner of nineteen years, but she still can't choose just one perfume.

Ordering is easy! Call us toll free or fax us to place your MC/VISA order.
You can also mail the order form below with payment to:
Cleis Press, 2246 Sixth St., Berkeley, CA 94710.

Buy 4 books, Get 1 *FREE**

ORDER FORM

QTY	TITLE	PRICE

SUBTOTAL	
SHIPPING	
SALES TAX	
TOTAL	

Add $3.95 postage/handling for the first book ordered and $1.00 for each additional book. Outside North America, please contact us for shipping rates. California residents add 9% sales tax. Payment in U.S. dollars only.

*** Free book of equal or lesser value. Shipping and applicable sales tax extra.**

Cleis Press • Phone: (800) 780-2279 • Fax: (510) 845-8001
orders@cleispress.com • www.cleispress.com
You'll find more great books on our website

Follow us on Twitter @cleispress • Friend/fan us on Fac